Thornes Classic Novels

THE TURN OF THE SCREW

by

HENRY JAMES

EDITED BY PAUL ROBERTS

SERIES EDITOR: JOHN SEELY

Stanley Thornes (Publishers) Ltd

The Turn of the Screw first published 1861.

This edition first published in 1996 by:
Stanley Thornes (Publishers) Ltd
Ellenborough House
Wellington Street
CHELTENHAM GL50 1YW
England

96 97 98 99 00 / 10 9 8 7 6 5 4 3 2 1

A catalogue record for this book is available from the British Library.

ISBN 0–7487–2424–9

Acknowledgements

The author and publishers are grateful to the following for permission
to reproduce illustrations and photographs:
Hulton Deutsch Collection, pages 2–3.

Illustrated by Dick Barton
Typeset by DP Press Ltd, Kent
Printed and bound in Great Britain at T J Press (Padstow) Ltd,
Cornwall

Contents

How to use this book

This edition of *The Turn of the Screw* is designed to help you get the most out of this story. It is presented in three parts:
- an introduction to the writer, the characters and the setting of the story;
- the story itself;
- the study guide – questions to help you understand what you have read.

INTRODUCTION

This contains an illustrated introduction to the writer, the characters and the setting of the story. You can read this material before starting the story, or you can leave it until later. If you get confused about people or places while reading the story, the introduction will make things clearer for you.

THE STORY

As well as the complete story itself, there are a number of other things to help you enjoy and understand it:
- at the beginning of each chapter, advice on what to look out for;
- on each page, a commentary that explains what is happening;
- on each page, notes that explain difficult words or expressions;
- 'fast forward' and 'rewind' sections (see below);
- illustrations of key moments;
- illustrations to help explain difficult words or expressions.

Fast forward/rewind sections

Some people like to read a story quickly to find out 'what happens next' missing out the less important sections. If you like to do this, the sections you can jump are marked. A 'fast forward' box (▶▶) tells you which page to jump to, a sign in the margin tells you where to start reading again, and a 'rewind' box (◀◀) tells you what was on the pages you have skipped.

STUDY GUIDE

This contains advice and activities to use while you are reading the story and after you have finished it. There is a more detailed explanation of how to use it at the beginning of the study guide itself.

Introduction

ABOUT THE WRITER

Henry James was born into a wealthy family in New York in 1843. He was the second eldest child and had three brothers and a sister. Henry's father was interested in philosophy and ideas. Henry and his elder brother William were strongly influenced by him. Henry took up his father's interests by becoming a novelist and William founded the first School of Psychology in New York.

In 1855, when Henry was 12, the family travelled to Europe and spent the next five years living in London, Paris, Geneva, Rome and other cities. In later years Henry was to return to Europe and spend much of his adult life living and writing in the cities he had first seen as a child.

The family returned to New York in 1860, a year before the beginning of the American Civil War, in which Henry's younger brothers fought. Henry was supposed to be studying law at Harvard University during the war years. In fact, he spent most of his time writing stories and taking his first steps towards becoming a novelist.

A photograph of New York taken in 1853

A photograph of Henry James in his study

From 1869 to 1877, Henry lived in Paris, Rome and London. He met famous French writers like Zola and Flaubert and the Russian novelist, Turgenev. During this time his first novels were published. *Roderick Hudson* and *The American* both deal with the differences and conflicts between the American and European cultures. This was to become the main theme of his work as a novelist.

In 1877 Henry moved to London but continued to travel and spend time with members of his family and his friends, one of whom was Robert Louis Stevenson. He wrote one of his most famous novels, *Portrait of a Lady* (1881), while he was staying in Venice. The idea for *The Turn of the Screw* (1896) came from a conversation Henry James had with the Archbishop of Canterbury. The Archbishop loved ghost stories and gave him the outline of the plot.

Henry James spent the final years of his life in Rye, Sussex. He became a British citizen in 1915 and died a year later in 1916. His sister-in-law crossed the Atlantic to America with his ashes, which were placed near the graves of his parents and his brothers.

POINTS OF VIEW

'It all depends on your point of view'

Statement by Michael, one of John's friends:
'David has been teasing John for ages. When John saw David walking past him with his jacket he grabbed him to try and get it back.'

Statement by Mr Ross, a teacher:
'David was minding his own business when John suddenly attacked him. It was completely uncalled for.'

1 Read the two views of the fight between John and David.
2 Imagine that the headteacher has asked to see Michael and Mr Ross to find out what has happened. Write a longer statement from each of them.
3 Which of the two witnesses is more reliable? Discuss this question and give reasons for your choice.

So, in this situation we see: ONE event and TWO interpretations of it.

At one point in *The Turn of the Screw*, the Governess, Flora (the little girl), and Mrs Grose (the housekeeper) are standing by a lake. The Governess says she can see the ghost of a woman across the water.

The story is not written in dialogue – the speeeches here have been taken out of the narrative.

In this situation there are THREE points of view:
The Governess who says that she sees a ghost and thinks that Flora *really* does as well;
Mrs Grose who says that *she* does not see the ghost and tries to protect Flora from what the Governess is saying;
Flora who says that she does *not* see a ghost and is frightened by the Governess's bullying.

The narrators

There are two narrators (storytellers) in *The Turn of the Screw*. In the Prologue, a character called Douglas says that he is going to read a story written by the Governess and told to him when he was a young man. He explains how the story was given to him when the Governess died. Douglas is one of a group of people gathered around a fire on Christmas Eve telling each other ghost stories. The Prologue is told from the point of view of another member of the group. After the Prologue, the story is told from the point of view of the Governess.

Starting a story in the present and then telling events which happened before the beginning of the story is called 'flashback'.

Prologue	Chapters 1–24
Narrated by one of a group listening to Douglas, who knew the Governess.	Narrated by the Governess in her written account of her story.

Timescale

The past   **The present**

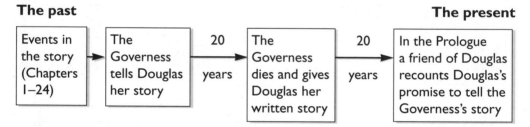

Events in the story (Chapters 1–24)	The Governess tells Douglas her story	20 years	The Governess dies and gives Douglas her written story	20 years	In the Prologue a friend of Douglas recounts Douglas's promise to tell the Governess's story

From Chapter 1 the Governess tells the story, but she may not be a reliable narrator. For instance, in the situation shown in the illustrations on the previous page there are two possibilities:

- The Governess really *does* see a ghost, and Flora is lying;
- The ghost is in the Governess's imagination, and Flora is telling the truth.

So, remember that the story is told from *one* point of view and that, as readers, we have to:

- decide how much of what the Governess tells us is the truth;
- listen to what the other characters say and decide if they are telling the truth.

It is sometimes difficult to decide *who* is telling the truth in this story. In the end… 'It all depends on YOUR point of view!'

THE SETTING

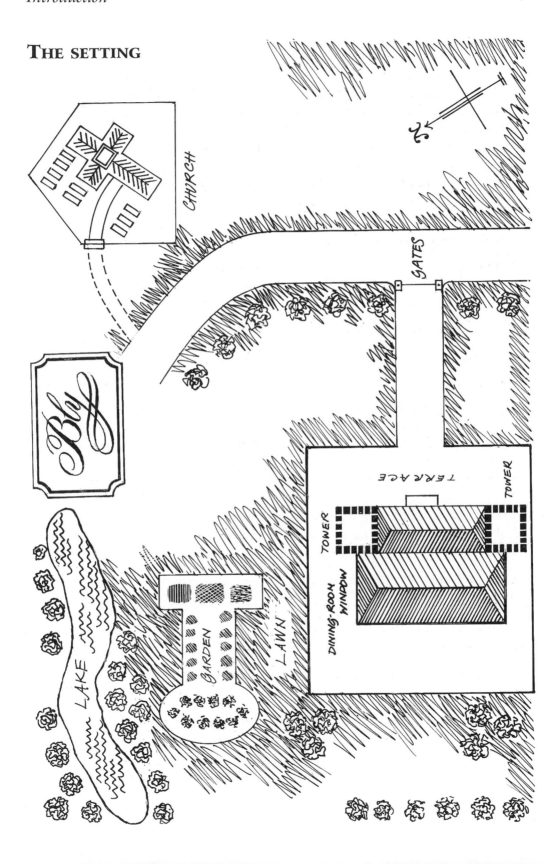

The staircase

The Governess's bedroom

The schoolroom

The dining-room window

The lawn and lake

THE CHARACTERS

The Governess and Miles

Mrs Grose and Flora

Peter Quint

Miss Jessel

The Uncle

Prologue

Look out for...
- **what Douglas says about the story.**
- **how Douglas comes to know the story.**
- **details about the Governess and the children.**

FAST FORWARD: to page 14

The story had held us, round the fire, sufficiently breathless, but except the obvious remark that it was gruesome, as on Christmas Eve in an old house a strange tale should essentially be, I remember no comment uttered till somebody happened to note it as the only case he had met in which such a visitation had fallen on a child. The case, I may mention, was that of an apparition in just such an old house as had gathered us for the occasion – an appearance, of a dreadful kind, to a little boy sleeping in the room with his mother and waking her up in the terror of it; waking her not to dissipate his dread and soothe him to sleep again, but to encounter also herself, before she had succeeded in doing so, the same sight that had shocked him. It was this observation that drew from Douglas – not immediately, but later in the evening – a reply that had the interesting consequence to which I call

COMMENTARY
A group of people are gathered around the fire on Christmas Eve in a large country house telling each other ghost stories. One of the stories involves a child seeing a ghost.

sufficiently breathless: excited
but except the obvious remark that it was gruesome: apart from the tale being frightening
essentially: really
apparition: ghost
dissipate: lessen

attention. Some one else told a story not particularly effective, which I saw he was not following. This I took for a sign that he had himself something to produce and that we should only have to wait. We waited in fact till two nights later; but the same evening, before we scattered, he brought out what was in his mind.

'I quite agree – in regard to Griffin's ghost, or whatever it was – that its appearing first to the little boy, at so tender an age, adds a particular touch. But it's not the first occurrence of its charming kind that I know to have been concerned with a child. If the child gives the effect another turn of the screw, what do you say to *two* children—?'

'We say of course,' somebody exclaimed, 'that two children give two turns! Also that we want to hear about them.'

I can see Douglas there before the fire, to which he had got up to present his back, looking down at this converser with his hands in his pockets. 'Nobody but me, till now, has ever heard. It's quite too horrible.' This was naturally declared by several voices to give the thing the utmost price, and our friend, with quiet art, prepared his triumph by turning his eyes over the rest of us and going on: 'It's beyond everything. Nothing at all that I know touches it.'

'For sheer terror?' I remember asking.

He seemed to say it wasn't so simple as that; to be really at a loss how to qualify it. He passed his hand over his eyes, made a little wincing grimace. 'For dreadful – dreadfulness!'

'Oh how delicious!' cried one of the women.

REWIND: …hear about them.
A group of people have gathered around the fireplace in a large country
house on Christmas Eve. They are telling each other ghost stories. One
of them, Douglas, offers to tell a story involving two children. The others are
immediately interested.

---

tender an age: young
occurrence: sort
gives the effect another turn of the screw:
    makes it a more exciting story
this converser: the person he is talking to
*give the thing the utmost price, and our
    friend, with quiet art, prepared his
    triumph:* made it more worth listening
    to and Douglas gets ready to tell his
    story
wincing grimace: pained expression

COMMENTARY
Douglas tells the others that he knows
a very frightening ghost story involving
two children.

He took no notice of her; he looked at me, but as if, instead of me, he saw
what he spoke of. 'For general uncanny ugliness and horror and pain.'

'Well then,' I said, 'just sit right down and begin.'

He turned round to the fire, gave a kick to a log, watched it an instant.
Then as he faced us again: 'I can't begin. I shall have to send to town.' There
was a unanimous groan at this, and much reproach; after which, in his
preoccupied way, he explained. 'The story's written. It's in a locked drawer – it
has not been out for years. I could write to my man and enclose the key; he
could send down the packet as he finds it.' It was to me in particular that he
appeared to propound this – appeared almost to appeal for aid not to hesitate.
He had broken a thickness of ice, the formation of many a winter; had had
his reasons for a long silence. The others resented postponement, but it was
just his scruples that charmed me. I adjured him to write by the first post and

COMMENTARY
Douglas says that the story
is written down and locked
away in his London house.
He offers to send for it.

uncanny: uncomfortably strange
town: London
unanimous: general
reproach: blame
my man: my servant
propound: say
*He had broken a thickness of ice, the formation of many
     a winter:* he had talked about a subject that he had
     not spoken about for a long time
resented postponement: objected to delay
scruples: hesitation
adjured: asked

to agree with us for an early hearing; then I asked him if the experience in question had been his own. To this his answer was prompt. 'Oh thank God, no!'

'And is the record yours? You took the thing down?'

'Nothing but the impression. I took that *here*' – he tapped his heart. 'I've never lost it.'

'Then your manuscript—?'

'Is in old faded ink and in the most beautiful hand.' He hung fire again. 'A woman's. She has been dead these twenty years. She sent me the pages in question before she died.' They were all listening now, and of course there was somebody to be arch, or at any rate to draw the inference. But if he put the inference by without a smile it was also without irritation. 'She was a most charming person, but she was ten years older than I. She was my sister's governess,' he quietly said. 'She was the most agreeable woman I've ever known in her position; she'd have been worthy of any whatever. It was long ago, and this episode was long before. I was at Trinity, and I found her at home on my coming down the second summer. I was much there that year – it was a beautiful one; and we had, in her off-hours, some strolls and talks in the garden – talks in which she struck me as awfully clever and nice. Oh yes; don't grin: I liked her extremely and am glad to this day to think she liked me too. If she hadn't she wouldn't have told me. She had never told any one. It wasn't simply that she said so, but that I knew she hadn't. I was sure; I could see. You'll easily judge why when you hear.'

'Because the thing had been such a scare?'

He continued to fix me. 'You'll easily judge,' he repeated: '*you* will.'

I fixed him too. 'I see. She was in love.'

He laughed for the first time. 'You *are* acute. Yes, she was in love. That is she *had* been. That came out – she couldn't tell her story without its coming out. I saw it, and she saw I saw it; but neither of us spoke of it. I remember the time and the place – the corner of the lawn, the shade of the great beeches and the long hot summer afternoon. It wasn't a scene for a shudder; but oh—!' He quitted the fire and dropped back into his chair.

COMMENTARY

Douglas's story was told to him by his sister's Governess when he was a young man on holiday from university. The Governess was ten years older than him and they had liked each other. At the time the Governess had been in love but we are not told with whom. (See the Introduction for information about how Douglas came to have a written version of the story.)

took the thing down: wrote the story down

hand: handwriting

somebody to be arch, or at any rate to draw the inference: someone teasingly thought that Douglas loved her

coming down the second summer: the second summer holiday of his time at university

off-hours: free time

acute: sharp witted

scene for a shudder: setting in which to feel scared

'You'll receive the packet Thursday morning?' I said.

'Probably not till the second post.'

'Well then; after dinner—'

'You'll all meet me here?' He looked us round again. 'Isn't anybody going?' It was almost the tone of hope.

'Everybody will stay!'

FAST FORWARD: to page 18

'*I* will – and *I* will!' cried the ladies whose departure had been fixed. Mrs Griffin, however, expressed the need for a little more light. 'Who was it she was in love with?'

'The story will tell,' I took upon myself to reply.

'Oh I can't wait for the story!'

'The story *won't* tell,' said Douglas; 'not in any literal vulgar way.'

'More's the pity then. That's the only way I ever understand.'

'Won't *you* tell, Douglas?' somebody else inquired.

He sprang to his feet again. 'Yes – to-morrow. Now I must go to bed. Goodnight.' And, quickly catching up a candlestick, he left us slightly bewildered. From our end of the great brown hall we heard his step on the stair; whereupon Mrs Griffin spoke. 'Well, if I don't know who she was in love with I know who *he* was.'

'She was ten years older,' said her husband.

'*Raison de plus* – at that age! But it's rather nice, his long reticence.'

'Forty years!' Griffin put in.

'With this outbreak at last.'

'The outbreak,' I returned, 'will make a tremendous occasion of Thursday night'; and every one so agreed with me that in the light of it we lost all attention for everything else. The last story, however incomplete and like the

---

COMMENTARY

Douglas goes to bed promising to read the story to them when it arrives from London. One of the party, Mrs Griffin, thinks that Douglas was in love with the Governess.

need for a little more light: more explanation
any literal vulgar way: any obvious way
bewildered: confused
Raison de plus: all the more reason
reticence: unwillingness to tell the story

mere opening of a serial, had been told; we handshook and 'candlestuck', as somebody said, and went to bed.

I knew the next day that a letter containing the key had, by the first post, gone off to his London apartments; but in spite of – or perhaps just on account of – the eventual diffusion of this knowledge we quite let him alone till after dinner, till such an hour of the evening in fact as might best accord with the kind of emotion on which our hopes were fixed. Then he became as communicative as we could desire, and indeed gave us his best reason for being so. We had it from him again before the fire in the hall, as we had had our mild wonders of the previous night. It appeared that the narrative he had promised to read us really required for a proper intelligence a few words of prologue. Let me say here distinctly, to have done with it, that this narrative, from an exact transcript of my own made much later, is what I shall presently give. Poor Douglas, before his death – when it was in sight – committed to me the manuscript that reached him on the third of these days and that, on the same spot, with immense effect, he began to read to our hushed little circle on the night of the fourth. The departing ladies who had said they would stay didn't, of course, thank heaven, stay: they departed, in consequence of arrangements made, in a rage of curiosity, as they professed, produced by the touches with which he had already worked us up. But that only made his little final auditory more compact and select, kept it, round the hearth, subject to a common thrill.

The first of these touches conveyed that the written statement took up the

▶▶ tale at a point after it had, in a manner, begun. The fact to be in possession of

---

REWIND: …in a manner, begun.

Douglas has gone to bed and the others are left with the impression that he was in love with the Governess. Douglas has hinted that *she* was also in love at the time of the story he is about to tell, which took place over forty years before this particular Christmas Eve. We learn that the narrator is telling *us* (the readers) the story after Douglas's death.

◀◀ ◀

---

candlestuck: took candles
diffusion: spreading
best accord with: best suit
wonders: questions
proper intelligence: real understanding
prologue: introduction
transcript: copy
committed: gave
professed: said
auditory: group of listeners

COMMENTARY
Douglas tells the party that he needs to give them some information before he reads the story to them.

was therefore that his old friend, the youngest of several daughters of a poor country parson, had at the age of twenty, on taking service for the first time in the schoolroom, come up to London, in trepidation, to answer in person an advertisement that had already placed her in brief correspondence with the advertiser. This person proved, on her presenting herself for judgement at a house in Harley Street that impressed her as vast and imposing – this prospective patron proved a gentleman, a bachelor in the prime of life, such a figure as had never risen, save in a dream or an old novel, before a fluttered anxious girl out of a Hampshire vicarage. One could easily fix his type; it never, happily, dies out. He was handsome and bold and pleasant, off-hand and gay and kind. He struck her, inevitably, as gallant and splendid, but what took her most of all and gave her the courage she afterwards showed was that he put the whole thing to her as a favour, an obligation he should gratefully incur. She figured him as rich, but as fearfully extravagant – saw him all in a glow of high fashion, of good looks, of expensive habits, of charming ways with women. He had for his town residence a big house filled with the spoils of travel and the trophies of the chase; but it was to his country home, an old family place in Essex, that he wished her immediately to proceed.

He had been left, by the death of his parents in India, guardian to a small nephew and a small niece, children of a younger, a military brother whom he had lost two years before. These children were, by the strangest of chances for a man in his position – a lone man without the right sort of experience or a grain of patience – very heavy on his hands. It had all been a great worry and, on his own part doubtless, a series of blunders, but he immensely pitied the poor chicks and had done all he could; had in particular sent them down to his other house, the proper place for them being of course the country, and kept them there from the first with the best people he could find to look after them, parting even with his own servants to wait on them and going down himself, whenever he might, to see how they were doing. The awkward thing was that they had practically no other relations and that his own affairs took up all his time. He had put them in possession of Bly, which was healthy and

COMMENTARY

When the Governess was 20 she travelled to London from her home in Hampshire to meet her future employer. He was a handsome and rich young man who wanted her to go to Bly, his country house in Essex, to look after his nephew and niece who had been left in his care following the deaths of their parents, his younger brother and his sister-in-law.

taking service: being employed as a Governess
trepidation: fear
prospective patron: possible employer
prime of life: young
fix: describe
off-hand and gay: carefree
an obligation he should gratefully incur: he would be happy to owe her a favour in return
fearfully: very
spoils of travel and trophies of the chase: souvenirs and stuffed animals

secure, and had placed at the head of their little establishment – but belowstairs only – an excellent woman, Mrs Grose, whom he was sure his visitor would like and who had formerly been maid to his mother. She was now housekeeper and was also acting for the time as superintendent to the little girl, of whom, without children of her own, she was by good luck extremely fond. There were plenty of people to help, but of course the young lady who should go down as governess would be in supreme authority. She would also have, in holidays, to look after the small boy, who had been for a term at school – young as he was to be sent, but what else could be done? – and who, as the holidays were about to begin, would be back from one day to the other. There had been for the two children at first a young lady whom they had had the misfortune to lose. She had done for them quite beautifully – she was a most respectable person – till her death, the great awkwardness of which had, precisely, left no alternative but the school for little Miles. Mrs Grose, since then, in the way of manners and things, had done as she could for Flora; and there were, further, a cook, a housemaid, a dairy woman, an old pony, an old groom, and an old gardener, all likewise thoroughly respectable.

So far had Douglas presented his picture when someone put a question. 'And what did the former governess die of? Of so much respectability?'

Our friend's answer was prompt. 'That will come out. I don't anticipate.'

'Pardon me – I thought that was just what you *are* doing.'

'In her successor's place,' I suggested, 'I should have wished to learn if the office brought with it—'

'Necessary danger to life?' Douglas completed my thought. 'She did wish to learn, and she did learn. You shall hear to-morrow what she learnt. Meanwhile of course the prospect struck her as slightly grim. She was young, untried, nervous: it was a vision of serious duties and little company, of really great loneliness. She hesitated – took a couple of days to consult and consider. But the salary offered much exceeded her modest measure, and on a second interview she faced the music, she engaged.'

but belowstairs only: Mrs Grose was
   responsible for all the servants –
   those 'below stairs' – at Bly
formerly: before
superintendent: in charge of
untried: innocent, inexperienced
much exceeded her modest measure:
   was more money than she was
   used to having

COMMENTARY
The children had a governess before who died and so Miles, the boy, had been sent to boarding school and Flora, the girl, was being looked after by Mrs Grose, the housekeeper. The Governess knew that the job would be hard and lonely but agreed to take it, partly because it is well paid.

FAST FORWARD: to page 22

And Douglas, with this, made a pause that, for the benefit of the company, moved me to throw in—

'The moral of which was of course the seduction exercised by the splendid young man. She succumbed to it.'

He got up and, as he had done the night before, went to the fire, gave a stir to a log with his foot, then stood a moment with his back to us. 'She saw him only twice.'

'Yes, but that's just the beauty of her passion.'

A little to my surprise, on this, Douglas turned round to me. 'It *was* the beauty of it. There were others,' he went on, 'who hadn't succumbed. He told her frankly all his difficulty – that for several applicants the conditions had been prohibitive. They were somehow simply afraid. It sounded dull – it sounded strange; and all the more so because of his main condition.'

'Which was—?'

'That she should never trouble him – but never, never; neither appeal nor complain nor write about anything; only meet all questions herself, receive all moneys from his solicitor, take the whole thing over and let him alone. She promised to do this, and she mentioned to me that when, for a moment, disburdened, delighted, he held her hand, thanking her for the sacrifice, she already felt rewarded.'

'But was that all her reward?' one of the ladies asked.

'She never saw him again.'

'Oh!' said the lady; which, as our friend immediately again left us, was the only other word of importance contributed to the subject till, the next night, by the corner of the hearth, in the best chair, he opened the faded red cover of a thin old-fashioned gilt-edged album. The whole thing took indeed more

COMMENTARY

The Governess is told that she can have the job on condition that she never contacts the children's uncle. Several others have refused the job. Douglas tells his audience that, once she had accepted the uncle's terms, the Governess never saw him again.

seduction: attraction
succumbed: gave in
prohibitive: too difficult
disburdened: relieved

nights than one, but on the first occasion the same lady put another question. 'What's your title?'

'I haven't one.'

'Oh *I* have!' I said. But Douglas, without heeding me, had begun to read with a fine clearness that was like a rendering to the ear of the beauty of his ▶▶ author's hand.

REWIND: …author's hand.
Douglas has hinted that the Governess was in love with her employer whom she only met twice. Her employer says that she must never contact him about the children and that she must take all the decisions about them. We learn that several others had refused the job as it sounded dull and strange. Now Douglas begins to read aloud the Governess's story.

◀◀

---

heeding me: listening to me
rendering to the ear of the beauty of his author's hand: in a voice suitable to the Governess's beautiful writing

COMMENTARY
Finally, Douglas says that his story has no title and begins to read from the pages that have been locked up for so long in his London house.

Look out for...
- **your impressions of Bly.**
- **the Governess is looking forward to a 'happy and useful' life – what will make it so for her?**
- **the relationship between the Governess and Mrs Grose.**

FAST FORWARD: to page 26

I remember the whole beginning as a succession of flights and drops, a little see-saw of the right throbs and the wrong. After rising, in town, to meet his appeal I had all events a couple of very bad days – found all my doubts bristle again, felt indeed sure I had make a mistake. In this state of mind I spent the long hours of bumping swinging coach that carried me to the stopping-place at which I was to be met by a vehicle from the house. This convenience, I was told, had been ordered, and I found, toward the close of the June afternoon, a commodious fly in waiting for me. Driving at that hour, on a lovely day, through a country the summer sweetness of which served as a friendly welcome, my fortitude revived and, as we turned into the avenue, took a flight that was probably but a proof of the point to which it had sunk. I suppose I had expected, or had dreaded, something so dreary that what greeted me was a

COMMENTARY
The Governess's worries about the job she has accepted are put aside as she approaches Bly through lovely countryside on a sunny day in June.

flights and drops, a little see-saw of the right throbs and the wrong: moments of doubt and excitement as she thinks about her first job
convenience: carriage
commodious fly: large, open carriage
fortitude revived: strength returned

good surprise. I remember as a thoroughly pleasant impression the broad clear front, its open windows and fresh curtains and the pair of maids looking out; I remember the lawn and the bright flowers and the crunch of my wheels on the gravel and the clustered tree-tops over which the rooks circled and cawed in the golden sky. The scene had a greatness that made it a different affair from my own scant home, and there immediately appeared at the door, with a little girl in her hand, a civil person who dropped me as decent a curtsey as if I had been the mistress or a distinguished visitor. I had received in Harley Street a narrower notion of the place, and that, as I recalled it, made me think the proprietor still more of a gentleman, suggested that what I was to enjoy might be a matter beyond his promise.

I had no drop again till the next day, for I was carried triumphantly through the following hours by my introduction to the younger of my pupils. The little girl who accompanied Mrs Grose affected me on the spot as a creature too charming not to make it a great fortune to have to do with her. She was the most beautiful child I had ever seen, and I afterwards wondered why my

scant: poor
narrower notion: less favourable
   impression
proprietor: owner
drop: worry
affected: struck
a great fortune: a pleasure

COMMENTARY
The Governess likes the house and grounds at Bly and is made even happier when she meets Flora, whom she thinks is a beautiful child.

employer hadn't made more of a point to me of this. I slept little that night – I was too much excited; and this astonished me too, I recollect, remained with me, adding to my sense of the liberality with which I was treated. The large impressive room, one of the best in the house, the great state bed, as I almost felt it, the figured full draperies, the long glasses in which, for the first time, I could see myself from head to foot, all struck me – like the wonderful appeal of my small charge – as so many things thrown in. It was thrown in as well, from the first moment, that I should get on with Mrs Grose in a relation over which, on my way, in the coach, I fear I had rather brooded. The one appearance indeed that in this early outlook might have made me shrink again was that of her being so inordinately glad to see me. I felt within half an hour that she was so glad – stout simple plain clean wholesome woman – as to be positively on her guard against showing it too much. I wondered even then a little why she should wish *not* to show it, and that, with reflexion, with suspicion, might of course have made me uneasy.

But it was a comfort that there could be no uneasiness in a connexion with anything so beatific as the radiant image of my little girl, the vision of whose angelic beauty had probably more than anything else to do with the restlessness that, before morning, made me several times rise and wander about my room to take in the whole picture and prospect; to watch from my open window the faint summer dawn, to look at such stretches of the rest of the house as I could catch, and to listen, while in the fading dusk the first birds began to twitter, for the possible recurrence of a sound or two, less natural and not without but within, that I had fancied I heard. There had been a moment when I believed I recognised, faint and far, the cry of a child; there had been another when I found myself just consciously starting as at the passage, before my door, of a light footstep. But these fancies were not marked enough not to be thrown off, and it is only in the light, or the gloom, I should rather say, of other and subsequent matters that they now come back to me. To watch, teach, 'form' little Flora would too evidently be the making of a happy and useful life. It had been agreed between us downstairs that after this first

COMMENTARY

The Governess is pleased with the room she is given and relieved that she gets on well with Mrs Grose. She wonders why Mrs Grose is so pleased to see her. Waking early on her first morning she thinks she hears a child crying and footsteps at her door, but the prospect of teaching Flora puts these things out of her mind.

liberality: generosity
the great state bed: a large bed for
  important people
the figured full draperies: embroidered
  curtains around the bed
my small charge: Flora

inordinately: very
beatific: spiritually beautiful
radiant image…restlessness: Flora's beauty
  had made her restless
prospect: view
recurrence: repetition

occasion I should have her as a matter of course at night, her small white bed being already arranged, to that end, in my room. What I had undertaken was the whole care of her, and she had remained just this last time with Mrs Grose only as an effect of our consideration for my inevitable strangeness and her natural timidity. In spite of this timidity – which the child herself, in the oddest way in the world, had been perfectly frank and brave about, allowing it, without a sign of uncomfortable consciousness, with the deep sweet serenity indeed of one of Raphael's holy infants, to be discussed, to be imputed to her and to determine us – I felt quite sure she would presently like me. It was part of what I already liked Mrs Grose herself for, the pleasure I could see her feel in my admiration and wonder as I sat at supper with four tall candles and with my pupil, in a high chair and a bib, brightly facing me between them over bread and milk. There were naturally things that in Flora's presence could pass between us only as prodigious and gratified looks, obscure
▶▶ and round-about allusions.

    'And the little boy – does he look like her? Is he too so very remarkable?'

    One wouldn't, it was already conveyed between us, too grossly flatter a child. 'Oh Miss, *most* remarkable. If you think well of this one!' – and she stood there with a plate in her hand, beaming at our companion, who looked from one of us to the other with placid heavenly eyes that contained nothing to check us.

    'Yes; if I do—?'

REWIND: …round-about allusions.
The Governess has arrived at Bly and found it a pleasant place to be. Mrs Grose, the housekeeper, is very pleased to see her, but she tries not to show it too much. Flora, the little girl, is beautiful. The Governess has heard strange noises in her first night at Bly. It has been agreed that Flora will sleep in the same room as the Governess. As the three of them sit down to supper, the Governess questions Mrs Grose.

⏪

---

a matter of course: usually
as an effect of our consideration: because of
allowing: showing
uncomfortable consciousness: embarrassment
serenity: calm
Raphael: was a sixteenth-century Italian painter
imputed: given
prodigious: meaningful
obscure and round-about allusions: hints
too grossly: over

COMMENTARY
Flora's bed is moved into the Governess's room. The Governess asks Mrs Grose what Flora's brother is like.

'You *will* be carried away by the little gentleman!'

'Well, that, I think, is what I came for – to be carried away. I'm afraid, however,' I remember feeling the impulse to add, 'I'm rather easily carried away. I was carried away in London!'

I can still see Mrs Grose's broad face as she took this in. 'In Harley Street?'

'In Harley Street.'

'Well, Miss, you're not the first – and you won't be the last.'

'Oh I've no pretensions,' I could laugh, 'to being the only one. My other pupil, at any rate, as I understand, comes back to-morrow?'

'Not to-morrow – Friday, Miss. He arrives, as you did, by the coach, under care of the guard, and is to be met by the same carriage.'

I forthwith wanted to know if the proper as well as the pleasant and friendly thing wouldn't therefore be that on the arrival of the public conveyance I should await him with his little sister; a proposition to which Mrs Grose assented so heartily that I somehow took her manner as a kind of comforting pledge – never falsified, thank heaven! – that we should on every question be quite at one. Oh she was glad I was there!

What I felt the next day was, I suppose, nothing that could be fairly called a reaction from the cheer of my arrival; it was probably at the most only a slight oppression produced by a fuller measure of the scale, as I walked round them, gazed up at them, took them in, of my new circumstances. They had as it were, an extent and mass for which I had not been prepared and in the presence of which I found myself, freshly, a little scared not less than a little proud. Regular lessons, in this agitation, certainly suffered some wrong; I reflected that my first duty was, by the gentlest arts I could contrive, to win the child into the sense of knowing me. I spent the day with her out of doors; I arranged with her, to her great satisfaction, that it should be she, she only, who might show me the place. She showed it step by step and room by room and secret by secret, with droll delightful childish talk about it and with the result, in half an hour, of our becoming tremendous friends. Young as she was I was struck, throughout our little tour, with her confidence and courage,

COMMENTARY

The Governess admits her liking for the uncle to Mrs Grose who tells her that she is not the first to have fallen for him. It is agreed that Flora and the Governess should go and meet Miles at the coaching station when he returns from school for the holidays. The Governess asks Flora to give her a tour of Bly so that they can get to know each other.

forthwith: immediately
proposition: suggestion
assented: agreed
a slight oppression…of the scale:
    scared by the size of the house
Regular lessons…some wrong: it was
    difficult to give good lessons
    when the Governess felt like this
contrive: plan
droll: amusing

with the way, in empty chambers and dull corridors, on crooked staircases that made me pause and even on the summit of an old machicolated square tower that made me dizzy, her morning music, her disposition to tell me so many more things than she asked, rang out and led me on. I have not seen Bly since the day I left it, and I dare say that to my present older and more informed eyes it would show a very reduced importance. But as my little conductress, with her hair of gold and her frock of blue, danced before me round corners and pattered down passages, I had the view of a castle of romance inhabited by a rosy sprite, such a place as would somehow, for diversion of the young idea, take all colour out of story-books and fairy-tales. Wasn't it just a story-book over which I had fallen a-doze and a-dream? No; it was a big ugly antique but convenient house, embodying a few features of a building still older, half-displaced and half-utilised, in which I had the fancy of our being almost as lost as a handful of passengers in a great drifting ship. Well, I was strangely at the helm!

machicolated: machicolations are parapets on the
   outside of castle towers and walls, with holes in
   the floors through which boiling oil could be
   poured onto enemies
sprite: spirit
such a place…and fairy tales: a place that would make
   story-book castles look dull
half-displaced and half-utilised: half empty and unused

COMMENTARY
Flora shows the Governess all over the house which the Governess thought at the time was like a fairy castle. Looking back she realises that it was only a 'big ugly antique'.

2

Look out for…
- the uncle's letter. How does Mrs Grose react to it? What difficulties does it cause the Governess?
- information about the first Governess.

This came home to me when, two days later I drove over with Flora to meet, as Mrs Grose said, the little gentleman; and all the more for an incident that, presenting itself the second evening, had deeply disconcerted me. The first day had been, on the whole, as I have expressed, reassuring; but I was to see it wind up to a change of note. The postbag that evening – it came late – contained a letter for me which, however, in the hand of my employer, I found to be composed but of a few words enclosing another, addressed to himself, with a seal still unbroken. 'This, I recognise, is from the head-master, and the head-master's an awful

COMMENTARY
On the Governess's second day at Bly a letter arrives from the uncle. The envelope contains an unopened letter from Miles's headmaster.

disconcerted: troubled
The first day had been…to a change of note: the writer is indicating here that the comfort she received on the first day was changed by events in the evening

bore. Read him, please; deal with him; but mind you don't report. Not a word. I'm off!' I broke the seal with a great effort – so great a one that I was a long time coming to it, took the unopened missive at last up to my room and only attacked it just before going to bed. I had better have let it wait till morning, for it gave me a second sleepless night. With no counsel to take, the next day, I was full of distress; and it finally got so the better of me that I determined to open myself at least to Mrs Grose.

'What does it mean? The child's dismissed his school.'

She gave me a look that I remarked at the moment; then visibly, with a quick blankness, seemed to try to take it back. 'But aren't they all – ?'

'Sent home – yes. But only for the holidays. Miles may never go back at all.'

Consciously, under my attention, she reddened. 'They won't take him?'

'They absolutely decline.'

At this she raised her eyes, which she had turned from me; I saw them fill with good tears. 'What has he done?'

I cast about; then I judged best simply to hand her my document – which, however, had the effect of making her, without taking it, simply put her hands behind her. She shook her head sadly. 'Such things are not for me, Miss.'

My counsellor couldn't read! I winced at my mistake, which I attenuated as I could, and opened the letter again to repeat it to her; then, faltering in the act and folding it up once more, I put it back in my pocket. 'Is he really *bad*?'

The tears were still in her eyes. 'Do the gentlemen say so?'

'They go into no particulars. They simply express their regret that it should be impossible to keep him. That can have but one meaning.' Mrs Grose listened with dumb emotion; she forbore to ask me what this meaning might be; so that, presently, to put the thing with some coherence and with the mere aid of her presence to my own mind, I went on: 'That he's an injury to the others.'

At this, with one of the quick turns of simple folk, she suddenly flamed up. 'Master Miles! – *him* an injury?'

missive: letter
no counsel: no advice
open myself: tell
cast about: wondered how to explain
attenuated: overcame
with dumb emotion: quietly upset
forebore to ask: did not ask
with some coherence: clearly

COMMENTARY
The headmaster's letter says that Miles has been expelled but gives no particular reason for this. When she offers the letter to Mrs Grose, the Governess discovers that she cannot read.

There was such a flood of good faith in it that, though I had not yet seen the child, my very fears made me jump to the absurdity of the idea. I found myself, to meet my friend the better, offering it, on the spot, sarcastically. 'To his poor little innocent mates!'

'It's too dreadful,' cried Mrs Grose, 'to say such cruel things! Why, he's scarce ten years old.'

'Yes, yes; it would be incredible.'

She was evidently grateful for such a profession. 'See him, Miss, first. *Then* believe it!' I felt forthwith a new impatience to see him; it was the beginning of a curiosity that, all the next hours, was to deepen almost to pain. Mrs Grose was aware, I could judge, of what she had produced in me, and she followed it up with assurance. 'You might as well believe it of the little lady. Bless her,' she added the next moment – '*look* at her!'

I turned and saw that Flora, whom, ten minutes before, I had established in the schoolroom with a sheet of white paper, a pencil, and a copy of nice 'round O's', now presented herself to view at the open door. She expressed in her little way an extraordinary detachment from disagreeable duties, looking at me, however, with a great childish light that seemed to offer it as a mere result of the affection she had conceived for my person, which had rendered necessary that she should follow me. I needed nothing more than this to feel the full force of Mrs Grose's comparison, and, catching my pupil in my arms, covered her with kisses in which there was a sob of atonement.

None the less, the rest of the day, I watched for further occasion to approach my colleague, especially as, toward evening, I began to fancy she rather sought to avoid me. I overtook her, I remember, on the staircase; we went down together and at the bottom I detained her, holding her there with a hand on her arm. 'I take what you said to me at noon as a declaration that *you've* never known him to be bad.'

She threw back her head; she had clearly by this time, and very honestly, adopted an attitude. 'Oh never known him – I don't pretend *that*!'

I was upset again. 'Then you *have* known him—?'

COMMENTARY

Mrs Grose is shocked that Miles, a 10-year-old boy, should be accused of being 'an injury to the others'. Later the Governess asks Mrs Grose if she has ever known Miles to be 'bad'.

good faith: belief

profession: speech

with a great childish light…should follow me: the writer is saying that Flora had copied her 'O's not for the pleasure of the task but because of her devotion to the Governess

atonement: making up

'Yes indeed, Miss, thank God!'

On reflexion I accepted this. 'You mean that a boy who never is—?'

'Is no boy for *me*!'

I held her tighter. 'You like them with the spirit to be naughty?'

Then, keeping pace with her answer, 'So do I!' I eagerly brought out. 'But not to the degree to contaminate—'

'To contaminate?' – my big word left her at a loss.

I explained it. 'To corrupt.'

She stared, taking my meaning in; but it produced in her an odd laugh. 'And you afraid he'll corrupt *you*?' She put the question with such a fine bold humour that with a laugh, a little silly doubtless, to match her own, I gave way for the time to the apprehension of ridicule.

But the next day, as the hour for my drive approached, I cropped up in another place. 'What was the lady who was here before?'

'The last governess? She was also young and pretty – almost as young and almost as pretty, Miss, even as you.'

'Ah then I hope her youth and her beauty helped her!' I recollect throwing off. 'He seems to like us young and pretty!'

'Oh he *did*,' Mrs Grose assented: 'it was the way he liked every one!' She had no sooner spoken indeed than she caught herself up. 'I mean that's *his* way – the master's.'

I was struck. 'But of whom did you speak first?'

She looked blank, but she coloured. 'Why of *him*.'

'Of the master?'

'Of who else?'

There was so obviously no one else that the next moment I had lost my impression of her having accidentally said more than she meant; and I merely asked what I wanted to know. 'Did *she* see anything in the boy—?'

'That wasn't right? She never told me.'

I had a scruple, but I overcame it. 'Was she careful – particular?'

Mrs Grose appeared to try to be conscientious. 'About some things – yes.'

the degree to contaminate: enough to infect others

corrupt: be an evil influence

gave way...ridicule: admitted that this was a ridiculous idea

scruple: doubt

conscientious: fair

COMMENTARY

The Governess and Mrs Grose are both glad that Miles has been bad in the past but the Governess hopes that he has not been *too* bad. Mrs Grose teases her by asking if she is afraid Miles will be a bad influence on her. Mrs Grose goes on to say that the previous Governess had been young and pretty and that is how *he* had liked them. The Governess has the impression that she is not talking about the uncle but another man.

'But not about all?'

Again she considered. 'Well, Miss – she's gone. I won't tell tales.'

'I quite understand your feeling,' I hastened to reply; but I thought it after an instant not opposed to this concession to pursue: 'Did she die here?'

'No – she went off.'

I don't know what there was in this brevity of Mrs Grose's that struck me as ambiguous. 'Went off to die?' Mrs Grose looked straight out of the window, but I felt that, hypothetically, I had a right to know what your persons engaged for Bly were expected to do. 'She was taken ill, you mean, and went home?'

'She was not taken ill, so far as appeared, in this house. She left it, at the end of the year, to go home, as she said, for a short holiday, to which the time she had put in had certainly given her a right. We had then a young woman – a nursemaid who had stayed on and who was a good girl and clever; and *she* took the children altogether for the interval. But our young lady never came back, and at the very moment I was expecting her I heard from the master that she was dead.'

I turned this over. 'But of what?'

'He never told me! But please, Miss,' said Mrs Grose, 'I must get to my work.'

COMMENTARY

Mrs Grose says that the previous Governess left Bly to go home for a holiday and never returned. She goes on to say that the young woman had died but that she did not know how. Mrs Grose ends the conversation quickly.

not opposed…to pursue: the writer is indicating that it was all right to ask further questions

brevity: short answer

ambiguous: having two meanings

hypothetically: theoretically

3

Look out for...
- **the Governess's comments about her younger self.**
- **the change in the Governess's mood after her first sighting of the figure on the tower.**
- **the Governess's reactions to the figure on the tower.**

H er thus turning her back on me was fortunately not, for my just preoccupations, a snub that could check the growth of our mutual esteem. We met, after I had brought home little Miles, more intimately than ever on the ground of my stupefaction, my general emotion: so monstrous was I then ready to pronounce it that such a child as had now been revealed to me should be under an interdict. I was a little late on the scene of his arrival, and I felt, as he stood wistfully looking out for me before the door of the inn at which the coach had put him down, that I had seen him on the instant, without and within, in the great glow of freshness, the same positive fragrance of purity, in which I had from the first moment seen his little sister. He was incredibly beautiful, and Mrs Grose had put her finger on it: everything but a sort of passion of tenderness for him was swept away by his presence. What I then and there took him to my heart for was something divine that I have never found to the same degree in any child – his indescribable little air of knowing nothing in the world but love. It would have been impossible to carry a bad name with a greater sweetness of innocence, and by the time I had got

for my just preoccupations: for her reasonable suspicions
snub: rejection
mutual esteem: liking each other
stupefaction: amazement
under an interdict: accused of doing something wrong
on the instant: immediately
passion of tenderness: tender feelings

COMMENTARY
The Governess goes to meet Miles. She thinks he is a beautiful child and cannot understand why he has been expelled.

back to Bly with him I remained merely bewildered – so far, that is, as I was not outraged – by the sense of the horrible letter locked up in one of the drawers of my room. As soon as I could compass a private word with Mrs Grose I declared to her that it was grotesque.

She promptly understood me 'You mean the cruel charge—?'

'It doesn't live an instant. My dear woman, *look* at him!'

She smiled at my pretension to have discovered his charm. 'I assure you, Miss, I do nothing else! What will you say then?' she immediately added.

'In answer to the letter?' I had made up my mind. 'Nothing at all.'

'And to his uncle?'

I was incisive. 'Nothing at all.'

'And to the boy himself?'

I was wonderful. 'Nothing at all.'

She gave with her apron a great wipe to her mouth. 'Then I'll stand by you. We'll see it out.'

'We'll see it out!' I ardently echoed, giving her my hand to make it a vow.

She held me there a moment, then whisked up her apron again with her detached hand. 'Would you mind, Miss, if I used the freedom—'

'To kiss me? No!' I took the good creature in my arms and after we had embraced like sisters felt still more fortified and indignant.

FAST FORWARD: to page 37

This at all events was for the time: a time so full that as I recall the way it went it reminds me of all the art I now need to make it a little distinct. What I look back at with amazement is the situation I accepted. I had undertaken, with my companion, to see it out, and I was under a charm apparently that could smooth away the extent and the far and difficult connexions of such an effort. I was lifted aloft on a great wave of infatuation and pity. I found it

COMMENTARY
The Governess decides to do nothing about the headmaster's letter. Mrs Grose says that she will support her in this decision.

compass: get
a time so full…a little distinct: a time it is difficult to describe clearly
could smooth away…an effort: the writer is indicating that the charm of the children could make the Governess forget the problems of doing nothing about the headmaster's letter
infatuation: blind love

simple, in my ignorance, my confusion, and perhaps my conceit, to assume that I could deal with a boy whose education for the world was all on the point of beginning. I am unable even to remember at this day what proposal I framed for the end of his holidays and the resumption of his studies. Lessons with me indeed, that charming summer, we all had a theory that he was to have; but I now feel that for weeks the lessons must have been rather my own. I learnt something – at first certainly – that had not been one of the teachings of my small smothered life; learnt to be amused, and even amusing, and not to think for the morrow. It was the first time, in a manner, that I had known space and air and freedom, all the music of summer and all the mystery of nature. And then there was consideration – and consideration was sweet. Oh it was a trap – not designed but deep – to my imagination, to my delicacy, perhaps to my vanity; to whatever in me was most excitable. The best way to picture it all is to say that I was off my guard. They gave me so little trouble – they were of a gentleness so extraordinary. I used to speculate – but even this with a dim disconnectedness – as to how the rough future (for all futures are rough!) would handle them and might bruise them. They had the bloom of health and happiness; and yet, as if I had been in charge of a pair of little grandees, of princes of the blood, for whom everything, to be right, would have to be fenced about and ordered and arranged, the only form that in my fancy the after-years could take for them was that of a romantic, a really royal extension of the garden and the park. It may be of course above all that what suddenly broke into this gives the previous time a charm of stillness – that hush in which something gathers or crouches. The change was actually like the spring of a beast.

In the first weeks the days were long; they often, at their finest, gave me what I used to call my own hour, the hour when, for my pupils, tea-time and bed-time having come and gone, I had before my final retirement a small interval alone. Much as I liked my companions this hour was the thing in the day I liked most; and I liked it best of all when, as the light faded – or rather, I should say, the day lingered and the last calls of the last birds sounded, in a

---

what proposal I framed: what plan I made
consideration: the writer is referring to her thoughts
    about doing a good job and following the uncle's
    instructions
speculate: think about
a dim disconnectedness: vaguely
grandees: Spanish word meaning 'lords'
the only form…and the park: the writer is saying that
    the only future which would not harm the
    children would be if they could always live in a
    garden like the one at Bly

COMMENTARY
The Governess does not think about the consequences of the letter. Looking back, she cannot remember what plans she made for educating Miles at home after the holidays.

flushed sky, from the old trees – I could take a turn into the grounds and enjoy, almost with a sense of property that amused and flattered me, the beauty and dignity of the place. It was a pleasure at these moments to feel myself tranquil and justified; doubtless perhaps also to reflect that by my discretion, my quiet good sense and general high propriety, I was giving pleasure – if he ever thought of it! – to the person to whose pressure I had yielded. What I was doing was what he had earnestly hoped and directly asked of me, and that I *could*, after all, do it proved even a greater joy than I had expected. I daresay I fancied myself in short a remarkable young woman and took comfort in the faith that this would more publicly appear. Well, I needed to be remarkable to offer a front to the remarkable things that presently gave their first sign. ◀◀

It was plump, one afternoon, in the middle of my very hour: the children were tucked away and I had come out for my stroll. One of the thoughts that, as I don't in the least shrink now from noting, used to be with me in these wanderings was that it would be as charming as a charming story suddenly to meet someone. Someone would appear there at the turn of a path and would stand before me and smile and approve. I didn't ask more than that – I only asked that he should *know*; and the only way to be sure he knew would be to see it, and the kind light of it, in his handsome face. That was exactly present to me – by which I mean the face was – when, on the first of these occasions, at the end of a long June day, I stopped short on emerging from one of the plantations and coming into view of the house. What arrested me on the spot – and with a shock much greater than any vision had allowed for – was the sense that my imagination had, in a flash, turned real. He did stand there! – but high up, beyond the lawn and at the very top of the tower to which, on

---

REWIND: …gave their first sign.
The Governess, the children and Mrs Grose settle into a contented routine which includes a quiet time for the Governess, which she calls 'my own hour', after the children have gone to bed.

COMMENTARY
One afternoon the Governess is walking in the grounds and thinking about what a good job she is doing at Bly and how well she is carrying out her employer's instructions. She imagines meeting him and being given an approving smile. Suddenly she looks up to see the figure of a man standing on one of the two towers at the corners of the house.

with a sense of property: the Governess imagines that she owns Bly
tranquil and justified: calm and satisfied
my discretion…high propriety: being sensible and behaving correctly
offer a front: meet
plump: exactly
arrested: stopped
greater than any vision had allowed for: greater than if she had actually seen the uncle

that first morning, little Flora had conducted me. This tower was one of a pair – square incongruous crenellated structures – that were distinguished, for some reason, though I could see little difference, as the new and the old. They flanked opposite ends of the house and were probably architectural absurdities, redeemed in a measure indeed by not being wholly disengaged nor of a height too pretentious, dating, in their gingerbread antiquity, from a romantic revival that was already a respectable past. I admired them, had fancies about them for we could all profit in a degree, especially when they loomed through the dusk, by the grandeur of their actual battlements; yet it was not at such an elevation that the figure I had so often invoked seemed most in place.

It produced in me, this figure, in the clear twilight, I remember, two distinct gasps of emotion, which were, sharply, the shock of my first and that of my second surprise. My second was a violent perception of the mistake of my first: the man who met my eyes was not the person I had precipitately supposed. There came to me thus a bewilderment of vision of which, after these years, there is no living view that I can hope to give. An unknown man in a lonely place is a permitted object of fear to a young woman privately bred; and the figure that faced me was – a few more seconds assured me – as little any one

incongruous crenellated structures: towers with
   battlements that did not fit in with the rest of the
   building
were probably architectural…respectable past: although
   out of place the towers were not too big and had
   been added when medieval architecture was
   fashionable
yet it was not…most in place: she had not imagined
   her employer to be standing on the tower
perception: realisation
precipitately: too soon
bewilderment of vision: confusing sight
privately bred: with a sheltered upbringing

COMMENTARY
The Governess is shocked
to realise that the figure on
the tower is not the uncle.

else I knew as it was the image that had been in my mind. I had not seen it in Harley Street – I had not seen it anywhere. The place, moreover, in the strangest way in the world, had on the instant and by the very fact of its appearance become a solitude. To me at least, making my statement here with a deliberation with which I have never made it, the whole feeling of the moment returns. It was as if, while I took in what I did take in, all the rest of the scene had been stricken with death. I can hear again, as I write, the intense hush in which the sounds of evening dropped. The rooks stopped cawing in the golden sky and the friendly hour lost for the unspeakable minute all its voice. But there was no other change in nature, unless indeed it were a change that I saw with a stranger sharpness. The gold was still in the sky, the clearness in the air, and the man who looked at me over the battlements was as definite as a picture in a frame. That's how I thought, with extraordinary quickness, of each person he might have been and that he wasn't. We were confronted across our distance quite long enough for me to ask myself with intensity who then he was and to feel, as an effect of my inability to say, a wonder that in a few seconds more became intense.

The great question, or one of these, is afterwards, I know, with regard to certain matters, the question of how long they have lasted. Well this matter of mine, think what you will of it, lasted while I caught at a dozen possibilities, none of which made a difference for the better, that I could see, in there having been in the house – and for how long, above all? – a person of whom I was in ignorance. It lasted while I just bridled a little with the sense of how my office seemed to require that there should be no such ignorance and no such person. It lasted while this visitant, at all event – and there was a touch of the strange freedom, as I remember, in the sign of familiarity of his wearing no hat – seemed to fix me, from his position, with just the question, just the scrutiny through the fading light, that his own presence provoked. We were too far apart to call to each other, but there was a moment at which, at shorter range, some challenge between us, breaking the hush, would have been the right result of our straight mutual stare. He was in one of the angles, the one away

COMMENTARY
Everything around the Governess goes deathly still as she tries to work out the identity of the figure on the tower. She can only suppose that it is someone living in the house without her knowledge.

making my...never made it: writing about this event for the first time
bridled: objected
seemed to fix me...presence provoked: looked at the Governess as if to challenge her to ask who he was
our straight mutual stare: looking straight at each other

from the house, very erect, as it struck me, and with both hands on the ledge. So I saw him as I see the letters I form on this page; then, exactly, after a minute, as if to add to the spectacle, he slowly changed his place – passed, looking at me hard all the while, to the opposite corner of the platform. Yes, it was intense to me that during this transit he never took his eyes from me, and I can see at this moment the way his hand, as he went, moved from one of the crenellations to the next. He stopped at the other corner, but less long, and even as he turned away still markedly fixed me. He turned away; that was all I knew.

spectacle: sight
markedly: deliberately

COMMENTARY
As the figure moves around the tower, he is looking straight at the Governess.

Look out for...
- **the Governess's thoughts and behaviour in the days following her first sight of the figure.**
- **Miles and Flora's behaviour and its effect on the Governess.**
- **the second appearance of the figure and how this affects the Governess and Mrs Grose.**

It was not that I didn't wait, on this occasion, for more, since I was as deeply rooted as shaken. Was there a 'secret' at Bly – a mystery of Udolpho or an insane, an unmentionable relative kept in unsuspected confinement? I can't say how long I turned it over, or how long, in a confusion of curiosity and dread, I remained where I had had my collision; I only recall that when I re-entered the house darkness had quite closed in. Agitation, in the interval, certainly had held me and driven me, for I must, in circling about the place, have walked three miles; but I was to be later on so much more overwhelmed that this mere dawn of alarm was a comparatively human chill. The most singular part of it in fact – singular as the rest had been – was the part I became, in the hall, aware of in meeting Mrs Grose. This picture comes back to me in the general train – the impression, as I received it on my return, of the wide white panelled space, bright in the lamplight and with its portraits and red carpet, and of the good surprised look of my friend, which immediately told me she had missed me. It came to me straightway, under contact, that, with plain heartiness, mere relieved anxiety at my appearance,

COMMENTARY
The Governess wonders if the figure is a mad relative kept secretly in the house. She spends a long time walking in the grounds and returns to the house after dark. Mrs Grose is relieved to see her.

mystery of Udolpho: The Mysteries of Udolpho, published in 1794, is a story in which the heroine is surrounded by supernatural mysteries
unsuspected confinement: secret captivity
later on so much…human chill: compared to what happened later this meeting was only mildly frightening
singular: peculiar
train: memory

she knew nothing whatever that could bear upon the incident I had there ready for her. I had not suspected in advance that her comfortable face would pull me up, and I somehow measured the importance of what I had seen by my thus finding myself hesitate to mention it. Scarce anything in the whole history seems to me so odd as this fact that my real beginning of fear was one, as I may say, with the instinct of sparing my companion. On the spot, accordingly, in the pleasant hall and with her eyes on me, I, for a reason that I couldn't then have phrased, achieved an inward revolution – offered a vague pretext for my lateness and, with the plea of the beauty of the night and of the heavy dew and wet feet, went as soon as possible to my room.

Here it was another affair; here, for many days after, it was a queer affair enough. There were hours, from day to day – or at least there were moments, snatched even from clear duties – when I had to shut myself up to think. It wasn't so much yet that I was more nervous than I could bear to be as that I was remarkably afraid of becoming so; for the truth I had now to turn over was simply and clearly the truth that I could arrive at no account whatever of the visitor with whom I had been so inexplicably and yet, as it seemed to me, so intimately concerned. It took me little time to see that I might easily sound, without forms of inquiry and without exciting remark, any domestic complication. The shock I had suffered must have sharpened all my senses; I felt sure, at the end of three days and as the result of mere closer attention, that I had not been practised upon by the servants nor made the object of any 'game'. Of whatever it was that I knew nothing was known around me. There was but one sane inference: someone had taken a liberty rather monstrous. That was what, repeatedly, I dipped into my room and locked the door to say to myself. We had been, collectively, subject to an intrusion; some unscrupulous traveller, curious in old houses, had made his way in unobserved, enjoyed the prospect from the best point of view and then stolen out as he came. If he had given me such a bold hard stare, that was but a part of his indiscretion. The good thing, after all, was that we should surely see no more of him.

Scarce anything…sparing my companion: what really frightens the Governess is that she feels the need to protect Mrs Grose from what she has seen

an inward revolution: a change of mind

pretext: excuse

for the truth…intimately concerned: the Governess could think of no explanation for the visitor

practised upon: tricked

sane reference: sensible conclusion

COMMENTARY
The Governess does not tell Mrs Grose about the figure on the tower. In the following days she spends long hours in her room thinking about what had happened and comes to the conclusion that the man must have been a stranger who had an interest in old houses.

FAST FORWARD: to page 44

This was not so good a thing, I admit, as not to leave me to judge that what, essentially, made nothing else much signify was simply my charming work. My charming work was just my life with Miles and Flora, and through nothing could I so like it as through feeling that to throw myself into it was to throw myself out of my trouble. The attraction of my small charges was a constant joy, leading me to wonder afresh at the vanity of my original fears, the distaste I had begun by entertaining for the probable grey prose of my office. There was to be no grey prose, it appeared, and no long grind; so how could work not be charming that presented itself as daily beauty? It was all the romance of the nursery and the poetry of the schoolroom. I don't mean by this of course that we studied only fiction and verse; I mean that I can express no otherwise the sort of interest my companions inspired. How can I describe that except by saying that instead of growing deadly used to them – and it's a marvel for a governess: I call the sisterhood to witness! – I made constant fresh discoveries. There was one direction, assuredly, in which these discoveries stopped: deep obscurity continued to cover the region of the boy's conduct at school. It had been promptly given me, I have noted, to face that mystery without a pang. Perhaps even it would be nearer the truth to say that – without a word – he himself had cleared it up. He had made the whole charge absurd. My conclusion bloomed there with the real rose-flush of his innocence: he was only too fine and fair for the little horrid unclean school-world, and he had paid a price for it. I reflected acutely that the sense of such individual differences, such superiorities of quality, always, on the part of the majority – which could include even stupid sordid head-masters – turns infallibly to the vindictive.

Both the children had a gentleness – it was their only fault, and it never made Miles a muff – that kept them (how shall I express it?) almost

COMMENTARY
The Governess enjoys teaching the children and this takes her mind off what has happened. She decides that Miles was expelled because he was too good and pure for the ordinary life of his school.

This was not…my charming work: the writer is saying that the Governess's pleasure in her work made her forget about seeing the man more than the thought that they would not see him again

grey prose: dullness

long grind: hard work going on for a long time

I call the sisterhood to witness: all those who have been Governesses will agree

obscurity…conduct at school: uncertainty about what Miles had done at school

bloomed: grew

I reflected…to the vindictive: people who were individuals and not part of the crowd were always treated spitefully by the majority

muff: someone who is no good at sport or their school work

impersonal and certainly quite unpunishable. They were like those cherubs of the anecdote who had – morally at any rate – nothing to whack! I remember feeling with Miles in especial as if he had had, as it were, nothing to call even an infinitesimal history. We expect of a small child scant enough 'antecedents', but there was in this beautiful little boy something extraordinarily sensitive, yet extraordinarily happy, that, more than in any creature of his age I have seen, struck me as beginning anew each day. He had never for a second suffered. I took this as a direct disproof of his having really been chastised. If he had been wicked he would have 'caught' it, and I should have caught it by the rebound – I should have found the trace, should have felt the wound and the dishonour. I could reconstitute nothing at all, and he was therefore an angel. He never spoke of his school, never mentioned a comrade or a master; and I, for my part, was quite too much disgusted to allude to them. Of course I was under the spell, and the wonderful part is that, even at the time, I perfectly knew I was. But I gave myself up to it; it was an antidote to any pain, and I had more pains than one. I was in receipt in these days of disturbing letters from home, where things were not going well. But with this joy of my children what things in the world mattered? That was the question I used to put to my scrappy retirements. I was dazzled by their loveliness.

There was a Sunday – to get on – when it rained with such force and for so many hours that there could be no procession to church; in consequence of which, as the day declined, I had arranged with Mrs Grose that, should the evening show improvement, we would attend together the late service. The rain happily stopped, and I prepared for our walk, which, through the park and by the good road to the village, would be a matter of twenty minutes.

REWIND: …dazzled by their loveliness.
The Governess has overcome her horror at seeing the man in the tower by throwing herself into her work with the children. She cannot understand why so sweet a child as Miles has been expelled from school.

---

cherubs of the anecdote: story-book angels
infinitesimal: tiny
scant enough 'antecedents': few events in the past to spoil
chastised: punished
If he had been…the dishonour: if he had been naughty the Governess would have been aware of it in his later behaviour
reconstitute: see
allude: speak about
antidote: cure
scrappy retirements: short periods when she was alone

COMMENTARY
Miles never talks about his school and shows no sign of being punished there and so the Governess concludes that he could not have done anything wrong. The Governess forgets her worries about the man she has seen, the mystery of Miles's school and some bad news she has received from her home by being with the children, whom she finds beautiful and fascinating.

Coming downstairs to meet my colleague
in the hall, I remembered a pair of gloves
that had required three stitches and that
had received them – with a publicity
perhaps not edifying – while I sat with
the children at their tea, served on
Sundays, by exception, in that cold
clean temple of mahogany and brass,
the 'grown-up' dining-room. The gloves
had been dropped there, and I turned in
to recover them. The day was grey
enough, but the afternoon light still
lingered, and it enabled me, on crossing
the threshold, not only to recognise, on a

chair near the wide window, then closed, the articles I wanted, but to become
aware of a person on the other side of the window and looking straight in. One
step into the room had sufficed; my vision was instantaneous; it was all there.
The person looking straight in was the person who had already appeared to
me. He appeared thus again with I won't say greater distinctness, for that was
impossible, but with a nearness that represented a forward stride in our
intercourse and made me, as I met him, catch my breath and turn cold. He
was the same – he was the same, and seen, this time, as he had been seen
before, from the waist up, the window, though the dining-room was on the
ground floor, not going down to the terrace on which he stood. His face was
close to the glass, yet the effect of this better view was, strangely, just to show
me how intense the former had been. He remained but a few seconds – long
enough to convince me he also saw and recognised; but it was as if I had been
looking at him for years and had known him always. Something, however,
happened this time that had not happened before; his stare into my face,
through the glass and across the room, was as deep and hard as then, but it
quitted me for a moment during which I could still watch it, see it fix

COMMENTARY
Before going to church one
Sunday evening, the Governess
goes into the dining room to
fetch her gloves. She sees the
mysterious man staring at her
through the window.

edifying: welcome
in that cold clean temple of mahogany and brass: the
    writer is describing a typical Victorian dining
    room full of brass objects and heavy furniture
sufficed: had been enough
instantaneous: immediate
intercourse: relationship
quitted: left

successively several other things. On the spot there came to me the added shock of a *certitude* that it was not for me he had come. He had come for someone else.

The flash of this knowledge – for it was knowledge in the midst of dread – produced in me the most extraordinary effect, starting, as I stood there, a sudden vibration of duty and courage. I say courage because I was beyond all doubt already far gone. I bounded straight out of the door again, reached that of the house, got in an instant upon the drive and, passing along the terrace as fast as I could rush, turned a corner and came full in sight. But it was in sight of nothing now – my visitor had vanished. I stopped, almost dropped, with the real relief of this; but I took in the whole scene – I gave him time to reappear. I call it time, but how long was it? I can't speak to the purpose to-day of the *duration* of these things. That kind of measure must have left me: they couldn't have lasted as they actually appeared to me to last. The terrace and the whole place, the lawn and the garden beyond it, all I could see of the park, were empty with a great emptiness. There were shrubberies and big trees, but I

certitude: certainty
duration: length

COMMENTARY
The Governess becomes aware that the figure is looking for someone else. Dashing out of the room she runs around the side of the house to where the man was standing but he has vanished.

remember the clear assurance I felt that none of them concealed him. He was there or was not there: not there if I didn't see him. I got hold of this; then, instinctively, instead of returning as I had come, went to the window. It was confusedly present to me that I ought to place myself where he had stood. I did so; I applied my face to the pane and looked, as he had looked, into the room. As if, at this moment, to show me exactly what his range had been, Mrs Grose, as I had done for himself just before, came in from the hall. With this I had the full image of a repetition of what had already occurred. She saw me as I had seen my own visitant; she pulled up short as I had done; I gave her something of the shock that I had received. She turned white, and this made me ask myself if I had blanched as much. She stared, in short, and retreated just on *my* lines, and I knew she had then passed out and come round to me and that I should presently meet her. I remained where I was, and while I waited I thought of more things than one. But there's only one I take space to mention. I wondered why *she* should be scared.

COMMENTARY

As the Governess stands in the same place as the man and looks through the window, as he had done, Mrs Grose enters the dining room. When she sees the Governess she looks scared and runs out of the room. As the Governess waits for Mrs Grose to join her, she wonders why she should have looked so scared.

applied: put
blanched: gone white

Look out for...
- **the description of Peter Quint.**
- **details about the previous summer when the children's uncle and Quint were at Bly.**
- **Mrs Grose's attitude during her conversation with the Governess.**

O h she let me know as soon as, round the corner of the house, she loomed again into view. 'What in the name of goodness is the matter—?' She was now flushed and out of breath.

I said nothing till she came quite near. 'With me?' I must have made a wonderful face. 'Do I show it?'

'You're as white as a sheet. You look awful.'

I considered; I could meet on this, without scruple, any degree of innocence. My need to respect the bloom of Mrs Grose's had dropped, without a rustle, from my shoulders, and if I wavered for the instant it was not with what I kept back. I put out my hand to her and she took it; I held her hard a little, liking to feel her close to me. There was a kind of support in the shy heave of her surprise. 'You came for me for church, of course, but I can't go.'

'Has anything happened?'

'Yes. You must know now. Did I look very queer?'

'Through this window? Dreadful!'

I could meet...had dropped: the writer felt able to reply to any comments quite naturally, and without hesitation, because she no longer feels the need to protect Mrs Grose from what she has seen on the tower and through the window

COMMENTARY
Mrs Grose joins the Governess on the terrace outside the dining room. The Governess decides to tell Mrs Grose who she saw through the dining room window.

'Well,' I said, 'I've been frightened.' Mrs Grose's eyes expressed plainly that *she* had no wish to be, yet also that she knew too well her place not to be ready to share with me any marked inconvenience. Oh it was quite settled that she *must* share! 'Just what you saw from the dining-room a minute ago was the effect of that. What *I* saw – just before – was much worse.'

Her hand tightened. 'What was it?'

'An extraordinary man. Looking in.'

'What extraordinary man?'

'I haven't the least idea.'

Mrs Grose gazed round us in vain. 'Then where is he gone?'

'I know still less.'

'Have you seen him before?'

'Yes – once. On the old tower.'

She could only look at me harder. 'Do you mean he's a stranger?'

'Oh very much!'

'Yet you didn't tell me?'

'No – for reasons. But now that you've guessed—'

Mrs Grose's round eyes encountered this charge. 'Ah I haven't guessed!' she said very simply. 'How can I if *you* don't imagine?'

'I don't in the very least.'

'You've seen him nowhere but on the tower?'

'And on this spot just now.'

Mrs Grose looked round again. 'What was he doing on the tower?'

'Only standing there and looking down at me.'

She thought a minute. 'Was he a gentleman?'

I found I had no need to think. 'No.' She gazed in deeper wonder. 'No.'

'Then nobody about the place? Nobody from the village?'

'Nobody – nobody. I didn't tell you, but I made sure.'

She breathed a vague relief: this was, oddly, so much to the good. It only went indeed a little way. 'But if he isn't a gentleman—'

'What *is* he? He's a horror.'

COMMENTARY

The Governess begins to tell Mrs Grose about the figure on the tower and seeing the same man through the window of the dining room. She says that she does not know who he is but can tell that he is not a 'gentleman'.

she knew too well…marked inconvenience: Mrs Grose knew that it was her duty to share any trouble in the house with the Governess

'A horror?'

'He's – God help me if I know *what* he is!'

Mrs Grose looked round once more; she fixed her eyes on the duskier distance and then, pulling herself together, turned to me with full inconsequence. 'It's time we should be at church.'

'Oh I'm not fit for church!'

'It won't do *them*—!' I nodded at the house.

'The children?'

'I can't leave them now.'

'You're afraid—?'

I spoke boldly. 'I'm afraid of *him*.'

Mrs Grose's large face showed me, at this, for the first time, the far-away faint glimmer of a consciousness more acute: I somehow made out in it the delayed dawn of an idea I myself had not given her and that was as yet quite obscure to me. It comes back to me that I thought instantly of this as something I could get from her; and I felt it to be connected with the desire she present showed to know more. 'When was it – on the tower?'

'About the middle of the month. At this same hour.'

'Almost at dark.' said Mrs Grose.

'Oh no, not nearly. I saw him as I see you.'

'Then how did he get in?'

'And how did he get out?' I laughed. 'I had no opportunity to ask him! This evening, you see,' I pursued, 'he has not been able to get in.'

'He only peeps?'

'I hope it will be confined to that!' She had now let go my hand; she turned away a little. I waited an instant; then I brought out: 'Go to church. Good-bye. I must watch.'

Slowly she faced me again. 'Do you fear for them?'

We met in another long look. 'Don't *you*?' Instead of answering she came nearer to the window and, for a minute, applied her face to the glass. 'You see how he could see,' I meanwhile went on.

with full inconsequence: completely changing the subject

I somehow made...obscure to me: Mrs Grose had some knowledge of the man before the Governess told her about him

COMMENTARY

The Governess says that she will not go to church but stay behind and watch for the man. She is afraid of what he might do to the children. Mrs Grose asks the Governess at what time she saw the man on the tower and seems to know something about him.

She didn't move. 'How long was he here?'

'Till I came out. I came to meet him.'

Mrs Grose at last turned round, and there was still more in her face. '*I* couldn't have come out.'

'Neither could I!' I laughed again. 'But I did come. I've my duty.'

'So have I mine,' she replied; after which she added: 'What's he like?'

'I've been dying to tell you. But he's like nobody.'

'Nobody?' she echoed.

'He has no hat.' Then seeing in her face that she already, in this, with a deeper dismay, found a touch of picture, I quickly added stroke by stroke. 'He has red hair, very red, close-curling, and a pale face, long in shape, with straight good features and little rather queer whiskers that are as red as his hair. His eyebrows are somehow darker; they look particularly arched and as if they might move a good deal. His eyes are sharp, strange – awfully; but I only know clearly that they're rather small and very fixed. His mouth's wide, and his lips are thin, and except for his little whiskers he's quite clean-shaven. He gives me a sort of sense of looking like an actor.'

'An actor!' It was impossible to resemble one less, at least, than Mrs Grose at that moment.

'I've never seen one, but so I suppose them. He's tall, active, erect,' I continued, 'but never – no, never! – a gentleman.'

My companion's face had blanched as I went on; her round eyes started and her mild mouth gaped. 'A gentleman?' she gasped, confounded stupefied: 'a gentleman *he*?'

'You know him, then?'

She visibly tried to hold herself. 'But he *is* handsome?'

I saw the way to help her. 'Remarkably!'

'And dressed—?'

'In somebody's clothes. They're smart, but they're not his own.'

She broke into a breathless affirmative groan. 'They're the master's!'

I caught it up. 'You *do* know him?'

COMMENTARY

The Governess describes the man to Mrs Grose and compares him to an actor. She goes on to say that his clothes did not seem to be his own. It becomes apparent that Mrs Grose knows who he is.

found a touch...stroke by stroke: she describes him as if she is painting a picture

a gentleman: someone who came from a wealthy and educated background

confounded stupefied: amazed

affirmative: positive

She faltered but a second. 'Quint!' she cried.

'Quint?'

'Peter Quint – his own man, his valet, when he was here!'

'When the master was?'

Gaping still, but meeting me, she pieced it all together. 'He never wore his hat, but he did wear – well, there were waistcoats missed! They were both here – last year. Then the master went, and Quint was alone.'

I followed, but halting a little. 'Alone?'

'Alone with *us*.' Then as from a deeper depth, 'In charge,' she added.

'And what became of him?'

She hung fire so long that I was still more mystified. 'He went too,' she brought out at last.

'Went where?'

Her expression, at this, became extraordinary. 'God knows where! He died.'

'Died?' I almost shrieked.

She seemed fairly to square herself, plant herself more firmly to express the wonder of it. 'Yes. Mr Quint's dead.

---

halting: not quite understanding
She hung fire: paused

COMMENTARY

Mrs Grose says that the man is Peter Quint, the uncle's manservant. Quint and the uncle were at Bly the previous summer, and when the uncle left Quint was left in charge. Finally, Mrs Grose tells the Governess that Quint is now dead.

6

Look out for...
- **the growing relationship between the Governess and Mrs Grose.**
- **the Governess's ideas about what Quint wants.**
- **Mrs Grose's attitude to Quint.**
- **information about Quint and the children's uncle.**
- **the Governess's and Flora's reactions to the 'person' across the lake.**

FAST FORWARD: to page 55

It took, of course, more than that particular passage to place us together in presence of what we had now to live with as we could, my dreadful liability to impressions of the order so vividly exemplified, and my companion's knowledge henceforth – a knowledge half consternation and half compassion – of that liability. There had been this evening, after the revelation that left me for an hour so prostrate – there had been for either of us no attendance on any service but a little service of tears and vows, of prayers and promises, a climax to the series of mutual challenges and pledges that had straightway ensued on our retreating together to the schoolroom and shutting ourselves up there to have everything out. The result of our having everything out was simply to reduce our situation to the last rigour of its elements. She herself had seen nothing, not the shadow of a shadow, and nobody in the house but the governess was in the governess's plight; yet she accepted without directly

COMMENTARY
The Governess and Mrs Grose shut themselves in the schoolroom and talk about the ghostly appearance of Quint. Mrs Grose says that she has never seen anything unusual at Bly.

to place us together…as we could: to realise that there were ghosts at Bly
my dreadful liability…exemplified: her ability to see ghosts
half consternation and half compassion: concern and pity
ensued: led to
the last rigour of its elements: its basic reality

impugning my sanity the truth as I gave it to her, and ended by showing me
on this ground an awestricken tenderness, a deference to my more than
questionable privilege, of which the very breath has remained with me as that
of the sweetest of human charities.

What was settled between us accordingly that night was that we thought
we might bear things together; and I was not even sure that in spite of her
exemption it was she who had the best of the burden. I knew at this hour, I
think, as well as I knew later, what I was capable of meeting to shelter my pupils;
but it took me some time to be wholly sure of what my honest comrade was
prepared for to keep terms with so stiff an agreement. I was queer company
enough – quite as queer as the company I received; but as I trace over what we
went through I see how much common ground we must have found in the one
idea that, by good fortune, *could* steady us. It was the idea, the second movement,
that led me straight out, as I may say, of the inner chamber of my dread. I could
take the air in the court, at least, and there Mrs Grose could join me. Perfectly
can I recall now the particular way strength came to me before we separated
for the night. We had gone over and over every feature of what I had seen.

'He was looking for someone else, you say – someone who was not you?'

'He was looking for little Miles.' A portentous clearness now possessed me.
'*That's* whom he was looking for.'

'But how do you know?'

'I know, I know, I know!' My exaltation grew. 'And *you* know, my dear!'

She didn't deny this, but I required, I felt, not even so much telling as that.
She took it up again in a moment. 'What if *he* should see him?'

'Little Miles?' That's what he wants!'

She looked immensely scared again. 'The child?'

'Heaven forbid! The man. He wants to appear to *them*.' That he might was
an awful conception, and yet somehow I could keep it at bay; which,
moreover, as we lingered there, was what I succeeded in practically proving. I
had an absolute certainty that I should see again what I had already seen, but
something within me said that by offering myself bravely as the sole subject of

---

impugning my sanity: thinking she is mad

a deference…privilege: a respect for her ability to see
    ghosts

I was not even…of the burden: even though Mrs Grose had
    not seen the ghost, she might have a more difficult time
    than the Governess

my honest comrade…agreement: Mrs Grose was capable of
    keeping her promise to help the Governess

the inner chamber of my dread…air in the court: the writer is
    comparing the Governess's worst fears of the ghost to
    an inner room and that talking to Mrs Grose has meant
    that she is less afraid and so has been led out of the
    inner chamber and into the courtyard of her fears

a portentous clearness: a clear sight of what is in the future

COMMENTARY
Mrs Grose accepts the
Governess's story and
they agree to help each
other. The Governess
thinks that Quint was
looking for Miles and
that he wants to appear
to both children.

awful conception: dreadful
    idea

keep it at bay: resist it

such experience, by accepting, by inviting, by surmounting it all, I should serve as an expiatory victim and guard the tranquillity of the rest of the household. The children in especial I should thus fence about and absolutely save. I recall one of the last things I said that night to Mrs Grose.

'It does strike me that my pupils have never mentioned—!'

She looked at me hard as I musingly pulled up. 'His having been here and the time they were with him?'

'The time they were with him, and his name, his presence, his history, in any way. They've never alluded to it.'

'Oh the little lady doesn't remember. She never heard or knew.'

'The circumstances of his death?' I thought with some intensity. 'Perhaps not. But Miles would remember – Miles would know.'

'Ah don't try him!' broke from Mrs Grose.

I returned her the look she had given me. 'Don't be afraid.' I continued to think. 'It *is* rather odd.'

'That he has never spoken of him?'

'Never by the least reference. And you tell me they were "great friends".'

'Oh it wasn't *him*!' Mrs Grose with emphasis declared. 'It was Quint's own fancy. To play with him, I mean – to spoil him.' She paused a moment; then she added: 'Quint was much too free.'

This gave me, straight from my vision of his face – *such* a face! – a sudden sickness of disgust. 'Too free with *my* boy?'

'Too free with everyone!' ◀◀

REWIND: …'Too free with everyone!'

The Governess and Mrs Grose have realised that Quint was looking for Miles as he stared through the window. The Governess thinks that as long as the ghost of Quint appears to her, then it will not appear to Miles and Flora. She also thinks it odd that the children have never mentioned their time with Quint. Mrs Grose has told the Governess that Quint was *over* friendly with everyone.

COMMENTARY
The Governess thinks that she will see Quint again and hopes that, by doing so, she will shield the rest of the household from his sight.
Mrs Grose says that Quint liked to think that he was 'great friends' with Miles.

an expiatory victim: a sacrifice
tranquillity: peace
musingly: thoughtfully
alluded: referred
fancy: idea
too free: over friendly

I forbore for the moment to analyse this description further than by the reflexion that a part of it applied to several of the members of the household, of the half-dozen maids and men who were still of our small colony. But there was everything, for our apprehension, in the lucky fact that no discomfortable legend, no perturbation of scullions, had ever, within any one's memory, attached to the kind old place. It had neither bad name nor ill fame, and Mrs Grose, most apparently, only desired to cling to me and to quake in silence. I even put her, the very last thing of all, to the test. It was when, at midnight, she had her hand on the schoolroom door to take leave. 'I *have* it from you then – for it's of great importance – that he was definitely and admittedly bad?'

'Oh not admittedly. *I* knew it – but the master didn't.'

'And you never told him?'

'Well, he didn't like tale-bearing – he hated complaints. He was terribly short with anything of that kind, and if people were all right to *him*—'

'He wouldn't be bothered with more?' This squared well enough with my impression of him: he was not a trouble-loving gentleman, nor so very particular perhaps about some of the company he himself kept. All the same, I pressed my informant. 'I promise you *I* would have told!'

She felt my discrimination. 'I daresay I was wrong. But really I was afraid.'

'Afraid of what?'

'Of things that man could do. Quint was so clever – he was so deep.'

I took this in still more than I probably showed. 'You weren't afraid of anything else? Not of his effect—?'

'His effect?' she repeated with a face of anguish and waiting while I faltered.

'On innocent little precious lives. They were in your charge.'

'No, they weren't in mine!' she roundly and distressfully returned. 'The master believed in him and placed him here because he was supposed not to be quite in health and the country air so good for him. So he had everything to say. Yes' – she let me have it – 'even about *them*.'

'Them – that creature?' I had to smother a kind of howl. 'And you could bear it?'

forbore: resisted

colony: community

perturbation of scullions: troublesome servants

She felt my discrimination: the writer is saying that the Governess makes Mrs Grose aware that she should have told the uncle

COMMENTARY

Mrs Grose knew that Quint was a bad influence at Bly but never told her master, the uncle. She explains this by saying that she was afraid of Quint and that the uncle would not have listened to her anyway. We learn that Quint was given a lot of authority in the house.

'No. I couldn't – and I can't now!' And the poor woman burst into tears.

A rigid control, from the next day, was, as I have said, to follow them; yet how often and how passionately, for a week, we came back together to the subject! Much as we had discussed it that Sunday night, I was, in the immediate later hours in especial – for it may be imagined whether I slept – still haunted with the shadow of something she had not told me. I myself had kept back nothing, but there was a word Mrs Grose had kept back. I was sure, moreover, by morning that this was not from a failure of frankness, but because on every side there were fears. It seems to me indeed, in raking it all over, that by the time the morrow's sun was high I had restlessly read into the facts before us almost all the meaning they were to receive from subsequent and more cruel occurrences. What they gave me above all was just the sinister figure of the living man – the dead one would keep a while! – and of the months he had continuously passed at Bly, which, added up, made a formidable stretch. The limit of this evil time had arrived only when, on the dawn of a winter's morning. Peter Quint was found, by a labourer going to early work, stone dead on the road from the village: a catastrophe explained – superficially at least – by a visible wound to his head; such a wound as might have been produced (and as, on the final evidence, *had* been) by a fatal slip, in the dark and after leaving the public-house, on the steepish icy slope, a wrong path altogether, at the bottom of which he lay. The icy slope, the turn mistaken at night and in liquor, accounted for much – practically, in the end and after the inquest and boundless chatter, for everything; but there had been matters in his life, strange passages and perils, secret disorders, vices more than suspected, that would have accounted for a good deal more.

I scarce know how to put my story into words that shall be a credible picture of my state of mind; but I was in these days literally able to find a joy in the extraordinary flight of heroism the occasion demanded of me. I now saw that I had been asked for a service admirable and difficult; and there would be a greatness in letting it be seen – oh in the right quarter! – that I could succeed where many another girl might have failed. It was an immense help to me – I

COMMENTARY
The Governess is sure there is something Mrs Grose has not told her about Quint. He died falling down a slope late at night, after he had just left the pub. There were rumours at the time of his death that he had led a wicked life.

frankness: honesty
restlessly read…cruel occurrences: given the facts a meaning that future events were to prove right
formidable stretch: long time
in liquor: drunk
boundless chatter: endless gossip
credible: believable

confess I rather applaud myself as I look back! – that I saw my response so strongly and so simply. I was there to protect and defend the little creatures in the world the most bereaved and the most lovable, the appeal of whose helplessness had suddenly become only too explicit, a deep constant ache of one's own engaged affection. We were cut off, really, together; we were united in our danger. They had nothing but me, and I – well, I had *them*. It was in short a magnificent chance. This chance presented itself to me in an image richly material. I was a screen – I was to stand before them. The more I saw the less they would. I began to watch them in a stifled suspense, a disguised tension, that might well, had it continued too long, have turned to something like madness. What saved me, as I now see, was that it turned to another matter altogether. I didn't last as suspense – it was superseded by horrible proofs. Proofs, I say, yes – from the moment I really took hold.

This moment dated from an afternoon hour that I happened to spend in the grounds with the younger of my pupils alone. We had left Miles indoors, on the red cushion of a deep window-seat; he had wished to finish a book, and I had been glad to encourage a purpose so laudable in a young man whose only defect was a certain ingenuity of restlessness. His sister, on the contrary, had been alert to come out, and I strolled with her half an hour, seeking the shade, for the sun was still high and the day exceptionally warm. I was aware afresh with her, as we went, of how, like her brother, she contrived – it was the charming thing in both children – to let me alone without appearing to drop me and to accompany me without appearing to oppress. They were never importunate and yet never listless. My attention to them all really went to seeing them amuse themselves immensely without me; this was a spectacle they seemed actively to prepare and that employed me as an active admirer. I walked in a world of their invention – they had no occasion whatever to draw upon mine; so that my time was taken only with being for them some remarkable person or thing that the game of the moment required and that was merely, thanks to my superior, my exalted stamp, a happy and highly distinguished sinecure. I forget what I was on the present occasion; I only

explicit: obvious

an image richly material: the writer is saying that the Governess had a very clear picture that she was a 'screen' between the children and Quint

laudable: praiseworthy

ingenuity of restlessness: ability to think of excuses not to sit still

oppress: cling

importunate: demanding

listless: bored

I walked in a world of their invention: she became part of their games

sinecure: a job in which she was paid to do nothing

COMMENTARY

The Governess gets great pleasure from the thought that she will triumph over the ghost and that the uncle will know that she has protected his niece and nephew. While Miles stays in the house, the Governess and Flora go for a walk.

remember that I was something very important and very quiet and that Flora was playing very hard. We were on the edge of the lake, and, as we had lately begun geography, the lake was the Sea of Azof.

Suddenly, amid these elements, I became aware that on the other side of the Sea of Azof we had an interested spectator. The way this knowledge gathered in me was the strangest thing in the world – the strangest, that is, except the very much stranger in which it quickly merged itself. I had sat down

with a piece of work – for I was something or other that could sit – on the old stone bench which overlooked the pond; and in this position I began to take in with certitude and yet without direct vision the presence, a good way off, of a third person. The old trees, the thick shrubbery, made a great and pleasant shade, but it was all suffused with the brightness of the hot still hour. There was no ambiguity in anything; none whatever at least in the conviction I from one moment to another found myself forming as to what I should see straight before me and across the lake as a consequence of raising my eyes. They were attached at this juncture to the stitching in which I was engaged, and I can feel once more the spasm of my effort not to move them till I should so have

Sea of Azof: part of the Black Sea in Russia

amid these elements: in the middle of imagining the lake was the Sea of Azof

suffused: covered

ambiguity: uncertainty

steadied myself as to be able to make up my mind what to do. There was an alien object in view – a figure whose right of presence I instantly and passionately questioned. I recollect counting over perfectly the possibilities, reminding myself that nothing was more nature, for instance, than the appearance of one of the men about the place, or even of a messenger, a postman or a tradesman's boy, from the village. That reminder had as little effect on my practical certitude as I was conscious – still even without looking – of its having upon the character and attitude of our visitor. Nothing was more natural than that these things should be the other things they absolutely were not.

Of the positive identity of the apparition I would assure myself as soon as the small clock of my courage should have ticked out the right second; meanwhile, with an effort that was already sharp enough, I transferred my eyes straight to little Flora, who, at the moment, was about ten yards away. My heart had stood still for an instant with the wonder and terror of the question whether she too would see; and I held my breath while I waited for what a cry from her, what some sudden innocent sign either of interest or of alarm, would tell me. I waited, but nothing came; then in the first place – and there is something more dire in this, I feel, than in anything I have to relate – I was determined by a sense that within a minute all spontaneous sounds from her had dropped; and in the second by the circumstance that also within the minute she had, in her play, turned her back to the water. This was her attitude when I at last looked at her – looked with the confirmed conviction that we were still, together, under direct personal notice. She had picked up a small flat piece of wood which happened to have in it a little hole that had evidently suggested to her the idea of sticking in another fragment that might figure as a mast and make the thing a boat. This second morsel, as I watched her, she was very markedly and intently attempting to tighten in its place. My apprehension of what she was doing sustained me so that after some seconds I felt I was ready for more. Then I again shifted my eyes – I faced what I had to face.

alien object: a stranger
right of presence: right to be there
That reminder had…absolutely were not: it was clear to her that the figure observing them was not one of the local people
the small clock…the right second: she was ready to look up
dire: dreadful
apprehension: understanding

COMMENTARY
The Governess notices that Flora has stopped her play chatter and turned her back to the water. Reassured by this she finally looks up and across the water.

7

Look out for...
- details about Miss Jessel.
- the Governess's thoughts about Flora.
- the relationship between Quint and Miss Jessel.

I got hold of Mrs Grose as soon after this as I could; and I can give no intelligible account of how I fought out the interval. Yet I still hear myself cry as I fairly threw myself into her arms: 'They *know* – it's too monstrous: they know, they know!'

intelligible: understandable

COMMENTARY
The Governess finds Mrs Grose and begins to tell her what she saw at the lake.

'And what on earth—?' I felt her incredulity as she held me.

'Why all that *we* know – and heaven knows what more besides!' Then as she released me I made it out to her, made it out perhaps only now with full coherency even to myself. 'Two hours ago, in the garden' – I could scarce articulate – 'Flora *saw*!'

Mrs Grose took it as she might have taken a blow in the stomach. 'She has told you?' she panted.

'Not a word – that's the horror. She kept it to herself! The child of eight, *that* child!' Unutterable still for me was the stupefaction of it.

Mrs Grose of course could only gape the wider. 'Then how do you know?'

'I was there – I saw with my eyes: saw she was perfectly aware.'

'Do you mean aware of *him*?'

'No – of *her*.' I was conscious as I spoke that I looked prodigious things, for I got the slow reflexion of them in my companion's face. 'Another person – this time; but a figure of quite as unmistakable horror and evil: a woman in black, pale and dreadful – with such an air also, and such a face! – on the other side of the lake. I was there with the child – quiet for the hour; and in the midst of it she came.'

'Came how – from where?'

'From where they come from! She just appeared and stood there – but not so near.'

'And without coming nearer?'

'Oh for the effect and the feeling she might have been as close as you!'

My friend, with an odd impulse, fell back a step. 'Was she someone you've never seen?'

'Never. But someone the child has. Someone *you* have.' Then to show how I had thought it all out: 'My predecessor – the one who died.'

'Miss Jessel?'

'Miss Jessel. You don't believe me?' I pressed.

She turned right and left in her distress. 'How can you be sure?'

This drew from me, in the state of my nerves, a flash of impatience. 'Then

---

incredulity: disbelief
made it out to her: explained
coherency: clearness
scarce articulate: hardly put it into words
Unutterable…of it: difficult to talk about the seriousness of it
prodigious: serious
predecessor: the person who came before her

COMMENTARY
The Governess guesses that the figure across the lake was the first governess, Miss Jessel. She says that, even though Flora did not admit it, she was aware that Miss Jessel was there. She is horrified by Flora's secrecy.

ask Flora – *she's* sure!' But I had no sooner spoken than I caught myself up. 'No, for God's sake, *don't*! She'll say she isn't – she'll lie!'

Mrs Grose was not too bewildered instinctively to protest. 'Ah how *can* you?'

'Because I'm clear. Flora doesn't want me to know.'

'It's only, then, to spare you.'

'No, no – there are depths, depths! The more I go over it the more I see in it, and the more I see in it the more I fear. I don't know what I *don't* see, what I *don't* fear!'

Mrs Grose tried to keep up with me. 'You mean you're afraid of seeing her again?'

'Oh no; that's nothing – now!' Then I explained. 'It's of *not* seeing her.'

But my companion only looked wan. 'I don't understand.'

'Why, it's that the child may keep it up – and that the child assuredly *will* – without my knowing it.'

At the image of this possibility Mrs Grose for a moment collapsed, yet presently to pull herself together again as from the positive force of the sense of what, should we yield an inch, there would really be to give away. 'Dear, dear – we must keep our heads! And after all, if she doesn't mind it—!' she even tried a grim joke. 'Perhaps she likes it!'

'Like *such* things – a scrap of an infant!'

'Isn't it just a proof of her blest innocence?' my friend bravely inquired.

She brought me, for the instant, almost round. 'Oh, we must clutch at *that* – we must cling to it! If it isn't a proof of what you say, it's a proof of – God knows what! For the woman's a horror of horrors.'

Mrs Grose, at this, fixed her eyes a minute on the ground; then at last raising them, 'Tell me how you know,' she said.

'Then you admit it's what she was?' I cried.

'Tell me how you know,' my friend simply repeated.

'Know? By seeing her! By the way she looked.'

'At you, do you mean – so wickedly?'

COMMENTARY

The Governess is afraid that Flora will go on seeing Miss Jessel without her knowing about it. Mrs Grose asks the Governess why she has described her as a 'horror of horrors'.

assuredly: certainly

from the positive force...give away: realising that if they gave way to the ghosts they would take over the children

'Dear me, no – I could have borne that. She gave me never a glance. She only fixed the child.'

Mrs Grose tried to see it. 'Fixed her?'

'Ah, with such awful eyes!'

She stared at mine as if they might really have resembled them. 'Do you mean of dislike?'

'God help us, no. Of something much worse.'

'Worse than dislike?' – this left her indeed at a loss.

'With a determination – indescribable. With a kind of fury of intention.'

I made her turn pale. 'Intention?'

'To get hold of her.' Mrs Grose – her eyes just lingering on mine – gave a shudder and walked to the window; and while she stood there looking out I completed my statement. '*That's* what Flora knows.'

After a little she turned round. 'The person was in black, you say?'

'In mourning – rather poor, almost shabby. But – yes – with extraordinary beauty.' I now recognised to what I had at last, stroke by stroke, brought the victim of my confidence, for she quite visibly weighed this. 'Oh handsome – very, very,' I insisted; 'wonderfully handsome. But infamous.'

She slowly came back to me. 'Miss Jessel – *was* infamous.' She once more took my hand in both her own, holding it as tight as if to fortify me against the increase of alarm I might draw from this disclosure. 'They were both infamous,' she finally said.

FAST FORWARD: to page 66

So for a little we faced it once more together; and I found absolutely a degree of help in seeing it now so straight. 'I appreciate,' I said, 'the great decency of your not having hitherto spoken; but the time has certainly come to give me the whole thing.' She appeared to assent to this, but still only in

borne: put up with

fixed: stared at

victim of my confidence: the writer means Mrs Grose to whom the Governess tells all her secrets

infamous: immoral

holding it as...disclosure: held her in case what was being said shocked her too much

hitherto: before

assent: agree

COMMENTARY

The Governess answers that Miss Jessel had stared at Flora 'with awful eyes' and that Flora had been aware that she had come to get her. At last, Mrs Grose admits that Quint and Miss Jessel had done something wrong at Bly and the Governess demands to know the whole story.

silence; seeing which I went on: 'I must have it now. Of what did she die? Come, there was something between them.'

'There was everything.'

'In spite of the difference—?'

'Oh of their rank, their condition' – she brought it woefully out. '*She* was a lady.'

I turned it over; I again saw. 'Yes – she was a lady.'

'And he so dreadfully below,' said Mrs Grose.

I felt that I doubtless needn't press too hard, in such company, on the place of a servant in the scale; but there was nothing to prevent an acceptance of my companion's own measure of my predecessor's abasement. There was a way to deal with that, and I dealt; the more readily for my full vision – on the evidence – of our employer's late clever good-looking 'own' man; impudent, assured, spoiled, depraved. 'The fellow was a hound.'

Mrs Grose considered as if it were perhaps a little a case for a sense of shades. 'I've never seen one like him. He did what he wished.'

'With *her*?'

'With them all.'

It was as if now in my friend's own eyes Miss Jessel had again appeared. I seemed at any rate for an instant to race their evocation of her as distinctly as I had seen her by the pond; and I brought out with decision: 'It must have been also what *she* wished!'

Mrs Grose's face signified that it had been indeed, but she said at the same time: 'Poor woman – she paid for it!'

'Then you do know what she died of?' I asked.

'No – I know nothing. I wanted not to know; I was glad enough I didn't; and I thanked heaven she was well out of this!'

'Yet you had, then, your idea—'

'Of her real reason for leaving? Oh yes – as to that. She couldn't have stayed. Fancy it here – for a governess! And afterwards I imagined – and I still imagine. And what I imagine is dreadful.'

COMMENTARY

The Governess and Mrs Grose talk about the social differences between Quint, a servant, and Miss Jessel, an educated lady. It is hinted that they had a relationship and that Miss Jessel had to leave because she was pregnant.

dreadfully below: from a lower social class

but there was nothing…predecessor's abasement: the Governess does not doubt Mrs Grose's judgement of Miss Jessel's shameful behaviour

depraved: immoral

Mrs Grose…sense of shades: Mrs Grose looked as if she were about to give a more detailed description than just that he was a 'hound'

evocation: description

'Not so dreadful as what *I* do.' I replied; on which I must have shown her –
as I was indeed but too conscious – a front of miserable defeat. It brought out
again all her compassion for me, and at the renewed touch of her kindness my
power to resist broke down. I burst, as I had the other time made her burst,
into tears, she took me to her motherly breast, where my lamentation
overflowed. 'I don't do it!' I sobbed in despair: 'I don't save or shield them! It's
▶▶ far worse than I dreamed. They're lost!'

REWIND: …They're lost!'
The Governess has demanded that Mrs Grose tells her about the
relationship between Quint and Miss Jessel. Mrs Grose has pointed out
the differences in their social class and hinted that the reason Miss Jessel had to
leave Bly was because she was pregnant.

◀◀

---

lamentation: sadness

COMMENTARY
The Governess realises that she does not shield the
children from the ghosts of Quint and Miss Jessel and,
worse than this, they are under the ghosts' influence.

Look out for...
- **ways in which Miles is said to be 'bad'.**
- **the relationship between Quint and Miles.**
- **how Miles and Flora helped in the relationship between Quint and Miss Jessel.**

FAST FORWARD: to page 70

What I had said to Mrs Grose was true enough: there were in the matter I had put before her depths and possibilities that I lacked resolution to sound; so that when we met once more in the wonder of it we were of a common mind about the duty of resistance to extravagant fancies. We were to keep our heads if we should keep nothing else – difficult indeed as that might be in the face of all that, in our prodigious experience, seemed least to be questioned. Late that night, while the house slept, we had another talk in my room; when she went all the way with me as to its being beyond doubt that I had seen exactly what I had seen. I found that to keep her thoroughly in the grip of this I had only to ask her how, if I had 'made it up', I came to be able to give, of each of the persons appearing to me, a picture disclosing, to the last detail, their special marks – a portrait on the exhibition of which she had

COMMENTARY
The Governess and Mrs Grose meet to go over the details of what has happened. Mrs Grose confirms that the Governess has seen Quint and Miss Jessel as the Governess has been able to describe them very accurately.

about the...fancies: not to exaggerate what had been seen
prodigious: meaningful

instantly recognised and named them. She wished, of course – small blame to her! – to sink the whole subject; and I was quick to assure her that my own interest in it had now violently taken the form of a search for the way to escape from it. I closed with her cordially on the article of the likelihood that with recurrence – for recurrence we took for granted – I should get used to my danger; distinctly professing that my personal exposure had suddenly become the least of my discomforts. It was my new suspicion that was intolerable; and yet even to this complication the later hours of the day had brought a little ease.

On leaving her, after my first outbreak, I had of course returned to my pupils, associating the right remedy for my dismay with that sense of their charm which I had already recognised as a resource I could positively cultivate and which had never failed me yet. I had simply, in other words, plunged afresh into Flora's special society and there become aware – it was almost a luxury! – that she could put her little conscious hand straight upon the spot that ached. She had looked at me in sweet speculation and then had accused me to my face of having 'cried'. I had supposed the ugly signs of it brushed away; but I could literally – for the time at all event – rejoice, under this fathomless charity, that they had not entirely disappeared. To gaze into the depths of blue of the child's eyes and pronounce their loveliness a trick of premature cunning was to be guilty of a cynicism in preference to which I naturally preferred to abjure my judgement and, so far as might be, my agitation. I couldn't abjure for merely wanting to, but I could repeat to Mrs Grose – as I did there, over and over, in the small hours – that with our small friends' voices in the air, their pressure on one's heart and their fragrant faces against one's cheek, everything fell to the ground but their incapacity and their beauty. It was a pity that, somehow, to settle this once for all, I had equally to re-enumerate the signs of subtlety that, in the afternoon, by the lake, had made a miracle of my show of self-possession. It was a pity to be obliged to reinvestigate the certitude of the moment itself and repeat how it had come to me as a revelation that the inconceivable communion I then

I closed with her cordially on the article: she spoke in a friendly way about the subject

distinctly professing: saying clearly

associating the right…their charm: the writer is saying that being with the children cures her anxiety about them

pronounce their loveliness…my judgement: she preferred not to think of Flora as cunning because that made her feel better

fathomless charity: great kindness

incapacity: the writer is suggesting that they are incapable of evil

to re-enumerate…self-possession: to relive the signs of secrecy which had made her calmness even more remarkable

a revelation that…a matter of habit: the Governess is amazed that what she thought was unbelievable was quite normal for Flora

COMMENTARY
The Governess is not afraid of seeing the ghosts again but is alarmed that the children might be communicating with them. When she is with the children she finds it hard to believe that they are wicked in any way.

surprised must have been for both parties a matter of habit. It was a pity I
should have had to quaver out again the reasons for my not having, in my
delusion, so much as questioned that the little girl saw our visitant even as I
actually saw Mrs Grose herself, and that she wanted, by just so much as she
did thus see, to make me suppose she didn't, and at the same time,
without showing anything, arrive at a guess as to whether I myself did! It
was a pity I needed to recapitulate the portentous little activities by which she
sought to divert my attention – the perceptible increase of movement, the
greater intensity of play, the singing, the gabbling of nonsense and the
invitation to romp.

Yet if I had not indulged, to prove there was nothing in it, in this review, I
should have missed the two or three dim elements of comfort that still
remained to me. I shouldn't for instance, have been able to asseverate to my
friend that I was certain – which was so much to the good – that *I* at least had
not betrayed myself. I shouldn't have been prompted, by stress of need, by
desperation of mind – I scarce know what to call it – to invoke such further
aid to intelligence as might spring from pushing my colleague fairly to the wall.
She had told me, bit by bit, under pressure, a great deal; but a small shifty spot
on the wrong side of it all still sometimes brushed my brow like the wing
of a bat, and I remember how on this occasion – for the sleeping house and
the concentration alike of our danger and our watch seemed to help – I felt the
importance of giving the last jerk to the curtain. 'I don't believe anything so
horrible,' I recollect saying; 'no, let us put it definitely, my dear, that I don't.
But if I did, you know, there's a thing I should require now, just without
sparing you the least bit more – oh not a scrap, come! – to get out of you.
What was it you had in mind when, in our distress, before Miles came back,
over the letter from his school, you said, under my insistence, that you didn't
pretend for him he hadn't literally *ever* been "bad"? He has *not*, truly, "ever", in
these weeks that I myself have lived with him and so closely watched him; he
has been an imperturbable little prodigy of delightful lovable goodness.
Therefore you might perfectly have made the claim for him if you had not, as

COMMENTARY
The Governess recalls all the ways Flora tried to distract her from looking at Miss
Jessel at the lake. She concludes that they must speak to each other regularly. She is
very uncertain about whether or not the children are innocent or whether they are
under the evil influence of the ghosts.

quaver out: say
she wanted…I myself did: Flora wanted to
  show the Governess that she did not
  see Miss Jessel and, at the same time,
  find out if the Governess did see her
perceptible: noticeable
asseverate declare
to invoke…to the wall: to get Mrs Grose

to tell her all she knows
but a small shifty spot…wing of a bat: there
  was still something the Governess did
  not know
I don't believe anything so horrible: the
  Governess does not believe, at this
  point, that the children are in touch with
  ghosts but she changes her mind later

▶▶ it happened, seen an exception to take. What was your exception, and to what passage in your personal observation of him did you refer?'

It was a straight question enough, but levity was not our note, and in any case I had before the grey dawn admonished us to separate got my answer. What my friend had had in mind proved immensely to the purpose. It was neither more nor less than the particular fact that for a period of several months Quint and the boy had been perpetually together. It was indeed the very appropriate item of evidence of her having ventured to criticise the propriety, to hint at the incongruity, of so close an alliance, and even to go so far on the subject as a frank overture to Miss Jessel would take her. Miss Jessel had, with a very high manner about it, requested her to mind her business, and the good woman had on this directly approached little Miles. What she had said to him, since I pressed, was that *she* liked to see young gentlemen not forget their station.

I pressed again, of course, the closer for that. 'You reminded him that Quint was only a base menial?'

'As you might say! And it was his answer, for one thing, that was bad.'

REWIND: …did you refer?'

Mrs Grose has told the Governess that she, too, knows about the ghosts, after at first trying to deny that they existed. The Governess is now worried that she does not shield the children from the ghosts and that they want, in some way, to get hold of the children.

She has realised that both Miles and Flora know all about them and suspects that Flora was pretending not to see Miss Jessel at the lake. The Governess has asked Mrs Grose what she meant when she said that she did not pretend that Miles had never been 'bad', as she thinks that this might have something to do with the ghosts.

levity: humour
admonished: told
immensely to the purpose: important to her enquiries about events at Bly
ventured to criticise…an alliance: been critical about a relationship between Miles and a servant
overture: appeal
base menial: servant

COMMENTARY
When she is asked how Miles had been bad, Mrs Grose describes the previous summer when Quint and Miss Jessel had been at Bly. Quint and Miles had spent a great deal of time together. She had objected about this to Miss Jessel but had been told to mind her own business.

'And for another thing?' I waited. 'He repeated your words to Quint?'

'No, not that, It's just what he *wouldn't!*' she could still impress on me. 'I was sure, at any rate,' she added, 'that he didn't. But he denied certain occasions.'

'What occasions?'

'When they had been about together quite as if Quint were his tutor – and a very grand one – and Miss Jessel only for the little lady. When he had gone off with the fellow, I mean, and spent hours with him.'

'He then prevaricated about it – he said he hadn't?' Her assent was clear enough to cause me to add in a moment: 'I see. He lied.'

'Oh!' Mrs Grose mumbled. This was a suggestion that it didn't matter; which indeed she backed up by a further remark. 'You see, after all, Miss Jessel didn't mind. She didn't forbid him.'

I considered. 'Did he put that to you as a justification?'

At this she dropped again. 'No, he never spoke of it.'

'Never mentioned her in connexion with Quint?'

She saw, visibly flushing, where I was coming out. 'Well, he didn't show anything. He denied,' she repeated; 'he denied.'

Lord, how I pressed her now! 'So that you could see he knew what was between the two wretches?'

'I don't know – I don't know!' the poor woman wailed.

'You do know, you dear thing,' I replied; 'only you haven't my dreadful boldness of mind, and you keep back, out of timidity and modesty and delicacy, even the impression that in the past, when you had, without my aid, to flounder about in silence, most of all made you miserable. But I shall get it out of you yet! There was something in the boy that suggested to you,' I continued, 'his covering and concealing their relation.'

'Oh he couldn't prevent—'

'Your learning the truth? I daresay! But, heavens,' I fell, with vehemence, a-thinking, 'what it shows that they must, to that extent, have succeeded in making of him!'

'Ah nothing that's not nice *now*!' Mrs Grose lugubriously pleaded.

COMMENTARY

Mrs Grose goes on to say that Miles never told her when he had been with Quint and never spoke about Quint and Miss Jessel to her. She realised that he was trying to hide something about their relationship. The Governess is concerned about the effect on Miles of being involved in this secret love affair.

prevaricated: hesitated
assent: agreement
justification: reason
even the impression…made you miserable: even the things that made you most unhappy
lugubriously: dismally

'I don't wonder you looked queer,' I persisted, 'when I mentioned to you the letter from his school!'

'I doubt if I looked as queer as you!' she retorted with homely force. 'And if he was so bad then as that comes to, how is he such an angel now?'

'Yes indeed – and if he was a fiend at school! How, how, how? Well,' I said in my torment 'you must put it to me again, though I shall not be able to tell you for some days. Only put it to me again!' I cried in a way that made my friend stare. 'There are directions in which I mustn't for the present let myself go.' Meanwhile I returned to her first example – the one to which she had just previously referred – of the boy's happy capacity for an occasional slip. 'If Quint – on your remonstrance at the time you speak of – was a base menial, one of the things Miles said to you, I find myself guessing, was you were another.' Again her admission was so adequate that I continued: 'And you forgave him that?'

'Wouldn't *you*?'

'Oh yes!' And we exchanged there, in the stillness a sound of the oddest amusement. Then I went on: 'At all events, while he was with the man—'

'Miss Flora was with the woman. It suited them all!'

It suited me too, I felt, only too well; by which I mean that it suited exactly the particular deadly view I was in the very act of forbidding myself to entertain. But I so far succeeded in checking the expression of this view that I will throw, just here, no further light on it than may be offered by the mention of my final observation to Mrs Grose. 'His having lied and been impudent are, I confess, less engaging specimens than I had hoped to have from you of the outbreak in him of the little natural man. Still,' I mused, 'they must do, for they make me feel more than ever that I must watch.'

It made me blush, the next minute, to see in my friend's face how much more unreservedly she had forgiven him than her anecdote struck me as pointing out to my own tenderness any way to do. This was marked when, at the schoolroom door, she quitted me. 'Surely you don't accuse *him*—'

'Of carrying on an intercourse that he conceals from me? Ah remember

---

boy's happy…slip: Miles's harmless wrong-doings
remonstrance: telling off
the particular…entertain: the 'deadly view' she is trying not to think about is that the children helped to keep the love affair a secret
engaging specimens: interesting evidence
the little natural man: human nature
to see in my…any way to do: Mrs Grose was able to forgive Miles more completely than the Governess

COMMENTARY
Listening to Mrs Grose, the Governess realises that Quint and Miss Jessel used the children as go-betweens in their secret love affair.

that, until further evidence, I now accuse nobody.' Then before shutting her out to go by another passage to her own place, 'I must just wait,' I wound up.

wound up: concluded

COMMENTARY
The Governess is determined to find out what has gone on between the four characters.

Look out for...
- the Governess's comments on her pupils.
- the way in which Henry James prepares us for another encounter with the ghost of Quint.

FAST FORWARD: to page 77

I waited and waited, and the days took as they elapsed something from my consternation. A very few of them, in fact, passing, in constant sight of my pupils, without a fresh incident, sufficed to give to grievous fancies and even to odious memories a kind of brush of the sponge. I have spoken of the surrender to their extraordinary childish grace as a thing I could actively promote in myself, and it may be imagined if I neglected now to apply at this source for whatever balm it would yield. Stranger than I can express, certainly, was the effort to struggle against my new lights. I would doubtless have been a greater tension still, however, had it not been so frequently successful. I used to wonder how my little charges could help guessing that I thought strange things about them; and the circumstance that these things only made them more interesting was not by itself a direct aid to keeping them in the dark. I trembled

the days took as they elapsed something from my consternation: she becomes less worried as the days go by
sufficed to give...of the sponge: managed to make her memories and thoughts less painful
balm: comfort
new lights: understanding of the situation
and the circumstance...in the dark: her strange thoughts about them did not help to keep them from knowing that she suspected them

COMMENTARY
Once again the Governess gets rid of her thoughts about the ghosts and the children's involvement with them by being in their company and enjoying their bright innocence.

less they should see that they *were* so immensely more interesting. Putting things at the worst, at all events, as in meditation I so often did, any clouding of their innocence could only be – blameless and foredoomed as they were – a reason the more for taking risks. There were moments when I knew myself to catch them up by an irresistible impulse and press them to my heart. As soon as I had done so I used to wonder – 'What will they think of that? Doesn't it betray too much?' It would have been easy to get into a sad wild tangle about how much I might betray; but the real account, I feel, of the hours of peace I could still enjoy was that the immediate charm of my companions was a beguilement still effective even under the shadow of the possibility that it was studied. For if it occurred to me that I might occasionally excite suspicion by the little outbreaks of my sharper passion for them, so too I remember asking if I mightn't see a queerness in the traceable increase of their own demonstrations.

They were at this period extravagantly and preternaturally fond of me; which, after all, I could reflect, was no more than a graceful response in children perpetually bowed down over and hugged. The homage of which they were so lavish succeeded in truth for my nerves quite as well as if I never appeared to myself, as I may say, literally to catch them at a purpose in it. They had never, I think, wanted to do so many things for their poor protectress; I mean – though they got their lessons better and better, which was naturally what would please her most – in the way of diverting, entertaining, surprising her; reading her passages, telling her stories, acting her charades, pouncing out at her, in disguises, as animals and historical characters, and above all astonishing her by the 'pieces' they had secretly got by heart and could interminably recite. I should never get to the bottom – were I to let myself go even now – of the prodigious private commentary, all under still more private correction, with which I these days overscored their full hours. They had shown me from the first a facility for everything, a general faculty which, taking a fresh start, achieved remarkable flights. They got their little tasks as if they loved them; they indulged, from the mere

---

COMMENTARY

The Governess notices that the children are more attentive to her and she thinks that their charm might be put on. She watches them for signs of leading a double life – being sweet and innocent to her and Mrs Grose while secretly talking to the dead lovers. The Governess also thinks that the children are watching *her* carefully.

meditation: thought

clouding: spoiling

For if it occurred to me…their own demonstrations: if the Governess's hugs were suspicious then the children's increased attention to her was also odd

preternaturally: unusually

The homage of which…purpose in it: their attention was as much a cure for her nerves as catching them being deliberately attentive would have been

interminably: endlessly

overscored: corrected

exuberance of the gift, in the most unimposed little miracles of memory. They not only popped out at me as tigers and as Romans, but as Shakespeareans, astronomers and navigators. This was so singularly the case that it had presumably much to do with the fact as to which, at the present day, I am at a loss for a different explanation: I allude to my unnatural composure on the subject of another school for Miles. What I remember is that I was content for the time not to open the question, and that contentment must have sprung from the sense of his perpetually striking show of cleverness. He was too clever for a bad governess, for a parson's daughter, to spoil; and the strangest if not the brightest thread in the pensive embroidery I just spoke of was the impression I might have got, if I had dared to work it out, that he was under some influence operating in his small intellectual life as a tremendous incitement.

If it was easy to reflect, however, that such a boy could postpone school, it was at least as marked that for such a boy to have been 'kicked out' by a school-master was a mystification without end. Let me add that in their company now – and I was careful almost never to be out of it – I could follow no scent very far. We lived in a cloud of music and affection and success and private theatricals. The musical sense in each of the children was of the quickest, but the elder in especial had a marvellous knack of catching and repeating. The schoolroom piano broke into all gruesome fancies; and when that failed there were confabulations in corners, with a sequel of one of them going out in the highest spirits in order to 'come in' as something new. I had had brothers myself, and it was no revelation to me that little girls could be slavish idolaters of little boys. What surpassed everything was that there was a little boy in the world who could have for the inferior age, sex and intelligence so fine a consideration. They were extraordinarily at one, and to say that they never either quarrelled or complained is to make the note of praise coarse for their quality of sweetness. Sometimes perhaps indeed (when I dropped into coarseness) I came across traces of little understandings between them by which one of them should keep me occupied while the other slipped away.

exuberance: excitement
unimposed: not asked for
pensive embroidery: the pattern of her thoughts
that he was under some...tremendous incitement: to avoid the subject of a new school, Miles is being careful to be good at his lessons
no scent: clues
catching: remembering
confabulations: plans
so fine a consideration: so sensitive an understanding
when I dropped into coarseness: the writer's intention here is to suggest that, sometimes, the Governess was realistic about the children

COMMENTARY
Because Miles is so good at his lessons, the Governess does not think about a new school for him. Both children are talented and good pupils but the Governess has the feeling that while one of them occupies her attention the other goes out to be with Quint or Miss Jessel.

There is a naïf side, I suppose, in all diplomacy; but if my pupils practised upon me it was surely with the minimum of grossness. It was all in the other quarter that, after a lull, the grossness broke out.

I find that I really hang back; but I must take my horrid plunge. In going on with the record of what was hideous at Bly I not only challenge the most liberal faith – for which I little care; but (and this is another matter) I renew what I myself suffered, I again push my dreadful way through it to the end. There came suddenly an hour after which, as I look back, the business seems to me to have been all pure suffering; but I have at least reached the heart of it, and the straightest road out is doubtless to advance. One evening – with nothing to lead up or prepare it – I felt the cold touch of the impression that had breathed on me the night of my arrival and which, much lighter then as I have mentioned, I should probably have made little of in memory had my subsequent sojourn been less agitated. I had not gone to bed; I sat reading by a couple of candles. There was a roomful of old books at Bly – last-century fiction some of it, which, to the extent of a distinctly deprecated renown, but never to so much as that of a stray specimen, had reached the sequestered home and appealed to the unavowed curiosity of my youth. I remember that the book I had in my hand was Fielding's *Amelia*; also that I was wholly awake. I recall further both a general conviction that it was horribly late and a particular objection to looking at my watch. I figure finally that the white

> **REWIND:** …grossness broke out.
> The Governess has realised that the children are being deliberately charming to avoid any questions about their contact with the ghosts.
> She is trying not to show that *she* knows that *they* know about the ghosts and hopes that her hugs and kisses will not show her worry for their safety. Flora and Miles are 'star' pupils and the Governess enjoys teaching them so much that she puts off thinking about a new school for Miles. She still cannot understand why he has been expelled.

COMMENTARY
The Governess is quite happy to accept that the children are 'using' her because they do it so sweetly. One night she is reading by candlelight on her own.

naïf side: unsuspecting
the minimum of grossness: not at all obvious
the most liberal faith: those willing to believe anything
I felt the cold touch…been less agitated: it is only because of horrible events that happened later that the noises the Governess heard on her first night became important
some of it…a stray specimen: some of the books were neither particularly good nor particularly bad
sequestered: private
unavowed: innocent
Fielding's Amelia: Amelia, published in 1752 – like the Governess, the heroine of Henry Fielding's novel has to overcome dangers and difficulties

curtain draping, in the fashion of those days, the head of Flora's little bed, shrouded, as I had assured myself long before, the perfection of childish rest. I recollect in short that though I was deeply interested in my author I found myself, at the turn of a page and with his spell all scattered, looking straight up from him and hard at the door of my room. There was a moment during which I listened, reminded of the faint sense I had had, the first night, of there being something undefinably astir in the house, and noted the soft breath of the open casement just move the half-drawn blind. Then, with all the marks of a deliberation that must have seemed magnificent had there been any one to admire it, I laid down my book, rose to my feet and, taking a candle, went straight out of the room and, from the passage, on which my light made little impression, noiselessly closed and locked the door.

I can say now neither what determined nor what guided me, but I went straight along the lobby, holding my candle high, till I came within sight of the tall window that presided over the great turn of the staircase. At this point I precipitately found myself aware of three things. They were practically simultaneous, yet they had flashes of succession. My candle, under a bold flourish, went out, and I perceived, by the uncovered window, that the yielding

dusk of earliest morning rendered it unnecessary. Without it, the next instant, I knew that there was a figure on the stair. I speak of sequences, but I required no lapse of seconds to stiffen myself for a third encounter with Quint. The apparition had reached the landing half-way up and was therefore on the spot nearest the window, where, at sight of me, it stopped short and fixed me exactly as it had fixed me from the tower and from the garden. He knew me as well as I knew him; and so,

precipitately: immediately
simultaneous: at the same time
succession: one event following another
I speak of sequences: putting things in the order they happened

in the cold faint twilight, with a glimmer in the high glass and another on the polish of the oak stair below, we faced each other in our common intensity. He was absolutely, on this occasion, a living detestable dangerous presence. But that was not the wonder of wonders; I reserve this distinction for quite another circumstance: the circumstance that dread had unmistakably quitted me and that there was nothing in me unable to meet and measure him.

I had plenty of anguish after that extraordinary moment, but I had, thank God, no terror. And he knew I hadn't – I felt myself at the end of an instant magnificently aware of this. I felt, in a fierce rigour of confidence, that if I stood my ground a minute I should cease – for the time at least – to have him to reckon with: and during the minute, accordingly, the thing was as human and hideous as a real interview: hideous just because it *was* human, as human as to have met alone, in the small hours, in a sleeping house, some enemy, some adventurer, some criminal. It was the dead silence of our long gaze at such close quarters that gave the whole horror, huge as it was, its only note of the unnatural. If I had met a murderer in such a place and at such an hour we still at least would have spoken. Something would have passed, in life, between us; if nothing had passed one of us would have moved. The moment was so prolonged that it would have taken but little more to make me doubt if even *I* were in life. I can't express what followed it save by saying that the silence itself – which was indeed in a manner an attestation of my strength – became the element into which I saw the figure disappear; in which I definitely saw it turn, as I might have seen the low wretch to which it had once belonged turn on receipt of an order, and pass, with my eyes on the villainous back that no hunch would have more disfigured, straight down the staircase and into the darkness in which the next bend was lost.

COMMENTARY

Even though the figure of Quint was evil and dangerous, the Governess is amazed to discover that she is not afraid of him. She stares back at him in silence and he turns and disappears into the darkness.

detestable: hateful
I reserve…circumstance: there was another remarkable fact
attestation: proof
low wretch: Quint

10

- Flora's reactions to the Governess when she is discovered out of bed.
- the Governess's ideas about what she is doing.
- the way in which this chapter builds up towards the surprise ending. How does Henry James achieve a sense of suspense?

I remained a while at the top of the stair, but with the effect presently of understanding that when my visitor had gone, he had gone; then I returned to my room. The foremost thing I saw there by the light of the candle I had left burning was that Flora's little bed was empty; and on this I caught my breath with all the terror that, five minutes before, I had been able to resist. I dashed at the place in which I had left her lying and over which – for the small silk counterpane and the sheets were disarranged – the white curtains had been deceivingly pulled forward; then my step, to my

foremost: first

COMMENTARY

The Governess returns to her room to find that Flora is not in her bed

unutterable relief, produced an answering sound: I noticed an agitation of the
window-blind, and the child, ducking down, emerged rosily from the other side
of it. She stood there in so much of her candour and so little of her
nightgown, with her pink bare feet and the golden glow of her curls. She
looked intensely grave, and I had never had such a sense of losing an
advantage acquired (the thrill of which had just been so prodigious) as on my
consciousness that she addressed me with a reproach – 'You naughty: where
have you been?' Instead of challenging her own irregularity I found myself
arraigned and explaining. She herself explained, for that matter, with the
loveliest eagerest simplicity. She had known suddenly as she lay there, that I
was out of the room, and had jumped up to see what had become of me. I had
dropped, with the joy of her reappearance, back into my chair – feeling then,
and then only, a little faint; and she had pattered straight over to me, thrown
herself upon my knee, given herself to be held with the flame of the candle full
in the wonderful little face that was still flushed with sleep. I remember closing
my eyes and instant, yielding, consciously, as before the excess of something
beautiful that shone out of the blue of her own. 'You were looking for me out
of the window?' I said. 'You thought I might be walking in the grounds?'

   'Well, you know, I thought someone was' – she never blanched as she
smiled out that at me.

   Oh how I looked at her now! 'And did you see any one?'

   'Ah *no*!' she returned almost (with the full privilege of childish
inconsequence) resentfully, though with a long sweetness in her little drawl of
the negative.

   At that moment, in the state of my nerves, I absolutely believed she lied;
and if I once more closed my eyes it was before the dazzle of the three or four
possible ways in which I might take this up. One of these for a moment
tempted me with such singular force that, to resist it, I must have gripped my
little girl with a spasm that, wonderfully, she submitted to without a cry or a
sign of fright. Why not break out at her on the spot and have it all over? – give
it to her straight in her lovely little lighted face? 'You see, you see, you *know*

COMMENTARY

Flora appears from behind the window
blinds and asks the Governess where
she has been. Flora says that she did
not see anyone out of the window but
the Governess thinks she is lying. The
Governess is tempted to ask Flora
how much she knows about the ghosts
of Quint and Miss Jessel.

unutterable: great
agitation: movement
candour: honesty
arraigned: accused
with the full…inconsequence: the writer is
   saying that children are not aware of
   the consequences of events and so have
   the privilege of not taking any
   responsibility for them

that you do and that you already quite suspect I believe it; therefore why not frankly confess it to me, so that we may at least live with it together and learn perhaps, in the strangeness of our fate, where we are and what it means?' This solicitation dropped, alas, as it came: if I could immediately have succumbed to it I might have spared myself – well, you'll see what. Instead of succumbing I sprang again to my feet, looked at her bed and took a helpless middle way. 'Why did you pull the curtain over the place to make me think you were still there?'

Flora luminously considered; after which, with her little divine smile: 'Because I don't like to frighten you!'

'But if I had, by your idea, gone out—?'

She absolutely declined to be puzzled; she turned her eyes to the flame of the candle as if the question were as irrelevant, or at any rate as impersonal, as Mrs Marcet or nine-times-nine. 'Oh but you know,' she quite adequately answered, 'that you might come back you dear, and that you *have!*' And after a little, when she had got into bed, I had, a long time, by almost sitting on her for the retention of her hand, to show how I recognised the pertinence of my return.

You may imagine the general complexion, from that moment, of my nights. I repeatedly sat up till I didn't know when; I selected moments when my room-mate unmistakably slept, and, stealing out, took noiseless turns in the passage. I even pushed as far as to where I had last met Quint. But I never met him there again, and I may as well say at once that I on no other occasion saw him in the house. I just missed, on the staircase, nevertheless, a different adventure. Looking down it from the top I once recognised the presence of a woman seated on one of the lower steps with her back presented to me, her body half-bowed and her head, in an attitude of woe, in her hands. I had been there but an instant, however, when she vanished without looking round at me. I knew, for all that, exactly what dreadful face she had to show; and I wondered whether, if instead of being above I had been below, I should have had the same nerve for going up that I had lately shown Quint. Well, there continued

solicitation: enquiring
succumbed: given in
luminously: beautifully
But if I had: the Governess is about to say that if she had gone out then there was no need to pull the curtain. Flora defends herself by saying that she pulled the curtain in case she came back
Mrs Marcet: Mrs Marcet wrote science textbooks for schoolchildren
retention: holding
to show how...return: the Governess stays with Flora to show that she appreciates her concern for her by closing the curtains

COMMENTARY
The Governess decides not to ask Flora about the ghosts, but with hindsight regrets this decision as she feels it would have saved her from events which came later. In the following nights the Governess leaves her room in search of the ghosts. Once, she sees the figure of Miss Jessel sitting sadly on the stairs where she had seen Quint.

to be plenty of call for nerve. On the eleventh night after my latest encounter with that gentleman – they were all numbered now – I had an alarm that perilously skirted it and that indeed, from the particular quality of its unexpectedness, proved quite my sharpest shock. It was precisely the first night during this series that, weary with vigils, I had conceived I might again without laxity lay myself down at my old hour. I slept immediately and, as I afterwards knew, till about one o'clock; but when I woke it was to sit straight up, as completely roused as if a hand had shaken me. I had left a light burning, but it was now out, and I felt an instant certainty that Flora had extinguished it. This brought me to my feet and straight, in the darkness, to her bed, which I found she had left. A glance at the window enlightened me further, and the striking of a match completed the picture.

The child had again got up – this time blowing out the taper, and had again, for some purpose of observation or response, squeezed in behind the blind and was peering out into the night. That she now saw – as she had not, I had satisfied myself, the previous time – was proved to me by the fact that she was disturbed neither by my reillumination nor by the haste I made to get into slippers and into a wrap. Hidden, protected, absorbed, she evidently rested on the sill – casement opened forward – and gave herself up. There was a great still moon to help her, and this fact had counted in my quick decision. She was face to face with the apparition we had met at the lake, and could now communicate with it as she had not then been able to do. What I, on my side, had to care for was, without disturbing her, to

perilously skirted: was dangerously near
vigils: watching at night
laxity: laziness
taper: candle

reach, from the corridor, some other window turned to the same quarter. I got to the door without her hearing me; I got out of it, closed it and listened, from the other side, for some sound from her. While I stood in the passage I had my eyes on her brother's door, which was but ten steps off and which, indescribably, produced in me a renewal of the strange impulse that I lately spoke of as my temptation. What if I should go straight in and march to *his* window? – what if, by risking to his boyish bewilderment a revelation of my motive, I should throw across the rest of the mystery the long halter of my boldness?

This thought held me sufficiently to make me cross to his threshold and pause again. I preternaturally listened; I figured to myself what might portentously be; I wondered if his bed were also empty and he also secretly at watch. It was a deep soundless minute, at the end of which my impulse failed. He was quiet; he might be innocent; the risk was hideous; I turned away. There was a figure in the grounds – a figure prowling for a sight, the visitor with whom Flora was engaged; but it wasn't the visitor most concerned with my boy. I hesitated afresh, but on other grounds and only a few seconds; then I had made my choice. There were empty rooms enough at Bly, and it was only a question of choosing the right one. The right one suddenly presented itself to me as the lower one – though high above the gardens – in the solid corner of the house that I have spoken of as the old Tower. This was a large square chamber, arranged with some state as a bedroom, the extravagant size of which made it so inconvenient that it had not for years, though kept by Mrs Grose in exemplary order, been occupied. I had often admired it and I knew my way about in it; I had only, after just faltering at the first chill gloom of it disuse, to pass across it and unbolt in all quietness one of the shutters. Achieving this transit I uncovered the glass without a sound and, applying my face to the pane, was able, in the darkness without being much less than within, to see that I commanded the right direction. Then I saw something more. The moon made the night extraordinarily penetrable and showed me on the lawn a person, diminished by distance, who stood there motionless and as if

quarter: direction
risking…motive: confusing Miles by telling him what she was doing
long halter of my boldness: the writer is comparing the Governess's control of the situation to the leather straps used as reins on dogs or horses
preternaturally: supernaturally
state: grandness
exemplary: exact and proper
faltering: hesitating
Achieving this transit: crossing the room
penetrable: easy to see in
diminished: made small

COMMENTARY
The Governess goes to look for a window in the house with the same view as her own so that she can see what Flora is looking at. She thinks Miles might be watching too and nearly goes into his room to find out. She finds a room with the right view in the old tower and crosses to look out of the window.

fascinated, looking up to where I had appeared – looking, that is, not so much straight at me as at something that was apparently above me. There was clearly another person above me – there was a person on the tower; but the presence on the lawn was not in the least what I had conceived and had confidently hurried to me. The presence on the lawn – I felt sick as I made it out – was poor little Miles himself.

COMMENTARY
The Governess sees, not Miss Jessel, as she had expected, but Miles on the lawn. He is looking at a point above her – at someone standing on the tower.

Look out for...
● what the Governess does after she has seen Miles on the lawn.
● Miles's explanation of what he was doing on the lawn.

FAST FORWARD: *to page 88*

It was not till late next day that I spoke to Mrs Grose; the rigour with which I kept my pupils in sight making it often difficult to meet her privately: the more as we each felt the importance of not provoking – on the part of the servants quite as much as on that of the children – any suspicion of a secret flurry or of a discussion of mysteries. I drew a great security in this particular from her mere smooth aspect. There was nothing in her fresh face to pass on to others the least of my horrible confidences. She believed me, I was sure, absolutely: if she hadn't I don't know what would have become of me, for I couldn't have borne the strain alone. But she was a magnificent monument to the blessing of a want of imagination, and if she could see in our little charges nothing but their beauty and amiability, their happiness and cleverness, she had no direct communication with the sources of my trouble. If they had been

rigour: strictness
great security: comfort
smooth aspect: calm face
But she was…want of imagination: Mrs Grose's lack of imagination, and the fact that she has not seen the ghosts, means that she can talk about the situation calmly

COMMENTARY
The next day the Governess is keen to keep what is happening a secret from the servants. Mrs Grose's steady and homely personality is a great help in presenting an outer calm.

at all visibly blighted or battered she would doubtless have grown, on tracing it back, haggard enough to match them; as matters stood, however, I could feel her, when she surveyed them with her large white arms folded and the habit of serenity in all her look, thank the Lord's mercy that if they were ruined the pieces would still serve. Flights of fancy gave place, in her mind, to a steady fireside glow, and I had already begun to perceive how, with the development of the conviction that – as time went on without a public accident – our young things could, after all, look out for themselves, she addressed her greatest solicitude to the sad case presented by the deputy-guardian. That, for myself, was a sound simplification: I could engage that, to the world, my face should tell no tales, but it would have been, in the conditions, an immense added worry to find myself anxious about hers.

At the hour I now speak of she had joined me, under pressure, on the terrace, where, with the lapse of the season, the afternoon sun was now agreeable; and we sat there together while before us and at a distance, yet within call if we wished, the children strolled to and fro in one of their most manageable moods. They moved slowly, in unison, below us, over the lawn, the boy, as they went, reading aloud from a story-book and passing his arm round his sister to keep her quite in touch. Mrs Grose watched them with positive placidity; then I caught the suppressed intellectual creak with which she conscientiously turned to take from me a view of the back of the tapestry. I had made her a receptacle of lurid things, but there was an odd recognition of my superiority – my accomplishments and my function – in her patience under my pain. She offered her mind to my disclosures as, had I wished to mix a witch's broth and proposed it with assurance, she would have held out a large clean saucepan. This had become thoroughly her attitude by the time that, in my recital of the events of the night, I reached the point of what Miles had said to me when, after seeing him, at such a monstrous hour, almost on the very spot where he happened now to be, I had gone down to bring him in; choosing then, at the window, with a concentrated need of not alarming the house, rather that method than any noisier process. I had left her meanwhile in

COMMENTARY

Mrs Grose is not worried about the children because she can see no sign of distress on their faces. She is more concerned about the Governess. The Governess and Mrs Grose are on the terrace watching the children on the lawn. The Governess begins to tell her about finding Miles on the lawn the night before.

serenity: calmness
if they were…still serve: if they were hurt by the experience they would still survive
Flights of fancy…glow: imagining horrid things gave way to calm thoughts
solicitude: concern
deputy-guardian: the Governess
placidity: calmness
then I caught…of the tapestry: unwillingly Mrs Grose listens to an account of the children which she does not like
a receptacle of lurid things: the Governess had told Mrs Gross strange and frightening things

little doubt of my small hope of representing with success even to her actual sympathy my sense of the real splendour of the little inspiration with which, after I had got him into the house, the boy met my final articulate challenge. As soon as I appeared in the moonlight on the terrace he had come to me as straight as possible; on which I had taken his hand without a word and led him, through the dark spaces, up the staircase where Quint had so hungrily hovered for him, along the lobby where I had listened and trembled, and so to his forsaken room.

Not a sound, on the way, had passed between us, and I had wondered – oh *how* I had wondered! – if he were groping about in his dreadful little mind for something plausible and not too grotesque. It would tax his invention certainly, and I felt, this time, over his real embarrassment, a curious thrill of triumph. It was a sharp trap for any game hitherto successful. He could play no longer at perfect propriety, nor could he pretend to it; so how the deuce would he get out of the scrape? There beat in me indeed, with the passionate throb of this question, an equal dumb appeal as to how the deuce *I* should. I was confronted at last, as never yet, with all the risk attached even now to sounding my own horrid note. I remember in fact that as we pushed into his little chamber, where the bed had not been slept in at all and the window, uncovered to the moonlight, make the place so clear that there was no need of striking a match – I remember how I suddenly dropped, sank upon the edge of the bed from the force of the idea that he must know how he really, as they

---

REWIND: …his forsaken room

The Governess and Mrs Grose are on the terrace watching the children on the lawn. They have decided not to discuss the situation in private for fear of alarming the servants.

  The Governess describes how, the previous night, she had gone out on to the lawn where Miles was standing in the moonlight and led him back into the house and up to his bedroom.

COMMENTARY

When Miles saw the Governess he went straight to her and allowed her to lead him upstairs. Catching Miles on the lawn pleases the Governess because she hopes that in explaining what he was doing he will confess his connection with the ghost of Quint.

---

articulate challenge: clear and precise
    question about what he had been doing
forsaken: empty
plausible: believable
grotesque: ridiculous
tax his invention: call on all his imagination

It was a sharp…successful: his
    embarrassment could cancel any of his
    successful schemes to deceive the
    Governess
propriety: good behaviour
how the deuce: how the devil

say, 'had' me. He could do what he liked, with all his cleverness to help him, so long as I should continue to defer to the old tradition of the criminality of those caretakers of the young who minister to superstitions and fears. He 'had' me indeed, and in a cleft stick; for who would ever absolve me, who would consent that I should go unhung, if, by the faintest tremor of an overture, I were the first to introduce into our perfect intercourse an element so dire? No, no: it was useless to attempt to convey to Mrs Grose, just as it is scarcely less so to attempt to suggest here, how, during our short stiff brush there in the dark, he fairly shook me with admiration. I was of course thoroughly kind and merciful; never, never yet had I placed on his small shoulders hands of such tenderness as those with which, while I rested against the bed, I held him there well under fire. I had no alternative but, in form at least, to put it to him.

'You must tell me now – and all the truth. What did you go out for? What were you doing there?'

I can still see his wonderful smile, the whites of his beautiful eyes and the uncovering of his clear teeth, shine to me in the dusk. 'If I tell you why, will you understand?' My heart, at this, leaped into my mouth. *Would* he tell me why? I found no sound on my lips to press it, and I was aware of answering only with a vague repeated grimacing nod. He was gentleness itself, and while I wagged my head at him he stood there more than ever a little fairy prince. It was high brightness indeed that gave me a respite. Would it be so great if he were really going to tell me? 'Well,' he said at last, 'just exactly in order that you should do this.'

'Do what?'

'Think me – for a change – *bad*!' I shall never forget the sweetness and gaiety with which he brought out the word, nor how, on top of it, he bent forward and kissed me. It was practically the end of everything. I met his kiss and I had to make, while I folded him for a minute in my arms, the most stupendous effort not to cry. He had given exactly the account of himself that permitted least my going behind it, and it was only with the effect of confirming

COMMENTARY	*'had'*: had an advantage over her
Miles explains his presence on the lawn to the Governess by saying that he did it to show that he could be bad if he wanted to be.	*He could do what he liked…an element so dire?*: as long as she did not accuse him directly of dealing with the ghosts, he could give any explanation and get away with it. If she did accuse him directly, and he really did know nothing about Quint, then this would put her in the wrong
	well under fire: under investigation
	respite: relief
	stupendous: great

my acceptance of it that, as I presently glanced about the room, I could say:

'Then you didn't undress at all?'

He fairly glittered in the gloom. 'Not at all. I sat up and read.'

'And when did you go down?'

'At midnight. When I'm bad I *am* bad!'

'I see, I see – it's charming. But how could you be sure I should know it?'

'Oh I arranged that with Flora.' His answers rang out with a readiness! 'She was to get up and look out.'

'Which is what she did do.' It was I who fell into the trap!

'So she disturbed you, and, to see what she was looking at, you also looked – you saw.'

'While you,' I concurred, 'caught your death in the night air!'

He literally bloomed so from this exploit that he could afford radiantly to assent. 'How otherwise should I have been bad enough?' he asked. Then, after another embrace, the incident and our interview closed on my recognition of all the reserves of goodness that, for his joke, he had been able to draw upon.

---

concurred: agreed

exploit: adventure

our interview closed…to draw upon:
   the Governess concludes that
   Miles's adventure has shown her
   that he is only a little boy who
   likes playing jokes and *not* that he
   is wicked and involved with
   supernatural events

COMMENTARY

Miles says that Flora had helped him by disturbing her sleep and staring out of the window so that the Governess would go and see what she was looking at. Faced with these believable explanations the Governess gives up trying to get to the truth.

12

Look out for...
- **the Governess's ideas about what the children are doing.**
- **the way in which Mrs Grose and the Governess refer to Quint and Miss Jessel.**

The particular impression I had received proved in the morning light, I repeat, not quite successfully presentable to Mrs Grose, though I re-enforced it with the mention of still another remark that he had made before we separated. 'It all lies in a half-a-dozen words.' I said to her, 'words that really settle the matter. "Think, you know, what I *might* do!" He threw that off to show me how good he is. He knows down to the ground what he "might do". That's what he gave them a taste of at school.'

'Lord, you do change!' cried my friend.

'I don't change – I simply make it out. The four, depend upon it, perpetually meet. If on either of these last nights you had been with either child you'd clearly have understood. The more I've watched and waited the more I've felt that if there were nothing else to make it sure it would be made so by the systematic silence of each. *Never*, by a slip of the tongue, have they so much as alluded to either of their old friends, any more than Miles has alluded to his expulsion. Oh yes, we may sit here and look at them, and they may show off to us there to their fill; but even while they pretend to be lost in their fairy-tale they're steeped in the vision of the dead restored to them. He's not reading to her,' I declared; 'they're talking of *them* – they're talking

---

COMMENTARY
The Governess is convinced that the two children meet the ghosts of Quint and Miss Jessel regularly. The proof of this for Mrs Grose lies in their deliberate silence on the subject of the dead couple and Miles's expulsion from school.

Think…might do: Miles seems to be hinting that he might do other bad things
perpetually: all the time
they're steeped…restored to them: the children are completely under the control of the ghosts

horrors! I go on, I know, as if I were crazy; and it's a wonder I'm not. What I've seen would have made *you* so; but it has only made me more lucid, made me get hold of still other things.'

My lucidity must have seemed awful, but the charming creatures who were victims of it, passing and repassing in their interlocked sweetness, gave my colleague something to hold on by; and I felt how tight she held as, without stirring in the breath of my passion, she covered them still with her eyes. 'Of what other things have you got hold?'

'Why, of the very things that have delighted, fascinated and yet, at bottom, as I now so strangely see, mystified and troubled me.' Their more than earthly beauty, their absolutely unnatural goodness. It's a game,' I went on; 'it's a policy and a fraud!'

'On the part of little darlings—?'

'As yet mere lovely babies? Yes, mad as that seems!' The very act of bringing it out really helped me to trace it – follow it all up and piece it all together. 'They haven't been good – they've only been absent. It has been easy to live with them because they're simply leading a life of their own. They're not mine – they're not ours. They're his and they're hers!'

'Quint's and that woman's?'

'Quint's and that woman's. They want to get to them.'

Oh how, at this, poor Mrs Grose appeared to study them! 'But for what?'

'For the love of all the evil that, in those dreadful days, the pair put into

---

lucid: clear

passing and repassing in their interlocked sweetness: going backwards and forwards in front of them sweetly wrapped in each other's arms

policy and a fraud: pretence or fake

COMMENTARY

The Governess thinks that the children have only pretended to be good and sweet but that in fact they are under the evil influence of Quint and Miss Jessel. Looking at Miles reading to his sister on the lawn, Mrs Grose finds this hard to believe.

them. And to ply them with that evil still, to keep up the work of demons, is what brings the others back.'

'Laws!' said my friend under breath. The exclamation was homely, but it revealed a real acceptance of my further proof of what, in the bad time – for there had been a worse even than this! – must have occurred. There could have been no such justification for me as the plain assent of her experience to whatever depth of depravity I found credible in our brace of scoundrels. It was in obvious submission of memory that she brought out after a moment: 'They *were* rascals! But what can they now do?' she pursued.

'Do?' I echoed so loud that Miles and Flora, as they passed at their distance, paused an instant in their walk and looked at us. 'Don't they do enough?' I demanded in a lower tone, while the children, having smiled and nodded and kissed hands to us, resumed their exhibition. We were held by it a minute; then I answered: 'They can destroy them!' At this my companion did turn, but the appeal she launched was a silent one, the effect of which was to make me more explicit. 'They don't know as yet quite how – but they're trying hard. They're seen only across, as it were, and beyond – in strange places and on high places, the top of towers, the roof of houses, the outside of windows, the further edge of pools; but there's a deep design, on either side, to shorten the distance and overcome the obstacle: so the success of the tempters is only a question of time. They've only to keep to their suggestions of danger.'

'For the children to come?'

'And perish in the attempt!' Mrs Grose slowly got up, and I scrupulously added: 'Unless, of course, we can prevent!'

Standing there before me while I kept my seat she visibly turned things over. 'Their uncle must do the preventing. He must take them away.'

'And who's to make him?'

She had been scanning the distance, but she now dropped on me a foolish face. 'You, Miss.'

'By writing to him that his house is poisoned and his little nephew and niece mad?'

COMMENTARY

Mrs Grose finally believes what her companion is saying. They both feel that the children will be in great danger unless they can stop the four meeting. Mrs Grose suggests that the Governess writes to the uncle to ask him to take the children away.

And to ply…evil still: to make them evil

in the bad time: when Quint and Miss Jessel were alive

There could have been…They were rascals: Mrs Grose agrees that the children are wicked because she knows how they lied and deceived her when Quint and Miss Jessel were alive

their exhibition: they think that the children are pretending to read on the lawn

explicit: clear

scrupulously: carefully

turned things over: thought about

scanning: looking at

'But if they *are*, Miss?'

'And if I am myself, you mean? That's charming news to be sent him by a person enjoying his confidence and whose prime undertaking was to give him no worry.'

Mrs Grose considered, following the children again. 'Yes, he do hate worry. That was the great reason—'

'Why those fiends took him in so long? No doubt, though his indifference must have been awful. As I'm not a fiend, at any rate, I shouldn't take him in.'

My companion, after an instant and for all answer, sat down again and grasped my arm. 'Make him at any rate come to you.'

I stared. 'To *me*?' I had a sudden fear of what she might do. '"Him"?'

'He ought to *be* here – he ought to help.'

I quickly rose and I think I must have shown her a queerer face than ever yet. 'You see me asking him for a visit?' No, with her eyes on my face she evidently couldn't. Instead of it even – as a woman reads another – she could see what I myself saw: his derision, his amusement, his contempt for the breakdown of my resignation at being left alone and for the fine machinery I had set in motion to attract his attention to my slighted charms. She didn't know – no one knew – how proud I had been to serve him and to stick to our terms; yet she none the less took the measure, I think, of the warning I now gave her. 'If you should so lose your head as to appeal to him for me—'

She was really frightened. 'Yes, Miss?'

'I would leave, on the spot, both him and you.'

derision: scorn
fine machinery…slighted charms:
   complicated plan to get his
   attention
took the measure: took notice

COMMENTARY

The Governess does not want to write to the uncle because she will then break his main condition that she should not contact him. She is in love with him but does not want to give him the impression that she is making up a story to get his attention. She threatens to leave if Mrs Grose contacts him.

13

Look out for...
- **the Governess's ideas about the children's communication with the ghosts of Quint and Miss Jessel.**
- **the Governess's desire to ask the children about the ghosts and her fears about mentioning them.**

FAST FORWARD: to page 100

It was all very well to join them, but speaking to them proved quite as much as ever an effort beyond my strength – offered, in close quarters, difficulties as insurmountable as before. This situation continued a month, and with new aggravations and particular notes, the note above all, sharper and sharper, of the small ironic consciousness on the part of my pupils. It was not, I am as sure to-day as I was sure then, my mere infernal imagination: it was absolutely traceable that they were aware of my predicament and that this strange relation made, in a manner, for a long time, the air in which we moved. I don't mean that they had their tongues in their cheeks or did anything vulgar, for that was not one of their dangers: I do mean, on the other hand, that the element of the unnamed and untouched became, between us, greater than any

COMMENTARY
While the Governess is sure about the children being in touch with the ghosts she knows that it would be difficult to ask about such a strange and frightening subject. She is convinced that she is not imagining the situation and feels sure that the children are plotting to keep the adults guessing about what they are doing.

new aggravations and particular notes: new worries and evidence

the small ironic consciousness: slightly humorous awareness of the Governess's problems

infernal: devilish

predicament: difficulty

unnamed and untouched: the writer is referring to the subject of Quint and Miss Jessel

other, and that so much avoidance couldn't have been made successful without a great deal of tacit arrangement. It was as if, at moments, we were perpetually coming into sight of subjects before which we must stop short, turning suddenly out of alleys that we perceived to be blind, closing with a little bang that made us look at each other – for, like all bangs, it was something louder than we had intended – the doors we had indiscreetly opened. All roads lead to Rome, and there were times when it might have struck us that almost every branch of study or subject of conversation skirted forbidden ground. Forbidden ground was the question of the return of the dead in general and of whatever, in especial, might survive, for memory, of the friends little children had lost. There were days when I could have sworn that one of them had, with a small invisible nudge, said to the other: 'She thinks she'll do it this time – but she *won't!*' To 'do it' would have been to indulge, for instance – and for once in a way – in some direct reference to the lady who had prepared them for my discipline. They had a delightful endless appetite for passages in my own history to which I had again and again treated them; they were in possession of everything that had ever happened to me, had had, with every circumstance the story of my smallest adventures and of those of my brothers and sisters and of the cat and the dog at home, as well as many particulars of the whimsical bent of my father, of the furniture and arrangement of our house and of the conversation of the old women of our village. There were things enough, taking one with another, to chatter about, if one went very fast and knew by instinct when to go round. They pulled with an art of their own the strings of my invention and my memory; and nothing else perhaps, when I thought of such occasions afterwards, gave me so the suspicion of being watched from under cover. It was in any case over *my* life, *my* past and *my* friends alone that we could take anything like our ease; a state of affairs that led them sometimes without the least pertinence to break out into sociable reminders. I was invited – with no visible connexion – to repeat afresh Goody Gosling's celebrated *mot* or to confirm the details already supplied as to the cleverness of the vicarage pony.

tacit arrangement: unspoken agreement

suddenly out of alleys…indiscreetly opened: the writer is describing the way in which they all avoided the subject of the ghosts

All roads lead to Rome: a proverb or well-known saying – here it means no matter what they talked about the subject of Quint and Miss Jessel was always present in their thoughts

passages in my own history: stories from her own family life

whimsical bent: a sense of humour

pulled with an art…strings of my invention: got her to tell stories

mot: French for 'word' – a celebrated *mot* is a memorable speech or saying

COMMENTARY

In the following days the Governess is aware that both she and the children are avoiding the subject of Quint and Miss Jessel. Miles and Flora fill any awkward silences with questions about the Governess's home and family. All the time, the Governess thinks that they are waiting for her to mention the servant and their first Governess.

It was partly at such junctures as these and partly at quite different ones that, with the turn my matters had now taken, my predicament, as I have called it, grew most sensible. The fact that the days passed for me without another encounter ought, it would have appeared, to have done something toward soothing my nerves. Since the light brush, that second night on the upper landing, of the presence of a woman at the foot of the stair, I had seen nothing, whether in or out of the house, that one had better not have seen. There was many a corner round which I expected to come upon Quint, and many a situation that, in a merely sinister way, would have favoured the appearance of Miss Jessel. The summer had turned, the summer had gone; the autumn had dropped upon Bly and had blown out half our lights. The place, with its grey sky and withered garlands, its bared spaces and scattered dead leaves, was like a theatre after the performance – all strewn with crumpled playbills. There were exactly states of the air, conditions of sound and of stillness, unspeakable impressions of the *kind* of ministering moment, that brought back to me, long enough to catch it, the feeling of the medium in which, that June evening out of doors, I had had my first sight of Quint, and in which too, at those other instants, I had, after seeing him through the window, looked for him in vain in the circle of shrubbery. I recognised the signs, the portents – I recognised the moment, the spot. But they remained unaccompanied and empty, and I continued unmolested: if unmolested one could call a young woman whose sensibility had, in the most extraordinary fashion, not declined but deepened. I had said in my talk with Mrs Grose on that horrid scene of Flora's by the lake – and had perplexed her by so saying – that it would from that moment distress me much more to lose my power than to keep it. I had then expressed what was vividly in my mind: the truth that, whether the children really saw or not – since, that is, it was not yet definitely proved – I greatly preferred, as a safeguard, the fulness of my own exposure. I was ready to know the very worst that was to be known. What I had then had an ugly glimpse of was that my eyes might be sealed just while theirs were most opened. Well, my eyes *were* sealed, it appeared, at present – a

COMMENTARY

As the summer passes and the autumn begins at Bly the Governess has the feeling that the ghosts are present and that the children are able to see them, even though she cannot.

junctures: points
predicament: difficulties
sensible: obvious
withered garlands: dying flowers
playbills: advertisements for the theatre
kind of ministering moment: time when the ghosts appeared
feeling of the medium: atmosphere
portents: signs
sensibility: awareness
as a safeguard…exposure: to see the ghosts so that she could keep an eye on them

consummation for which it seemed blasphemous not to thank God. There was, alas, a difficulty about that: I would have thanked him with all my soul had I not had in a proportionate measure this conviction of the secret of my pupils.

How can I retrace to-day the strange steps of my obsession? There were times of our being together when I would have been ready to swear that, literally, in my presence, but with my direct sense of it closed, they had visitors who were known and were welcome. Then it was that, had I not been deterred by the very chance that such an injury might prove greater than the injury to be averted, my exaltation would have broken out. 'They're here, they're here, you little wretches,' I would have cried, 'and you can't deny it now!' The little wretches denied it with all the added volume of their sociability and their tenderness, just in the crystal depths of which – like the flash of a fish in a stream – the mockery of their advantage peeped up. The shock had in truth sunk into me still deeper than I knew on the night when, looking out either for Quint or for Miss Jessel under the star, I had seen there the boy over whose rest I watched and who had immediately brought in with him – had straightway there turned on me – the lovely upward look with which, from the battlements above us, the hideous apparition of Quint had played. If it was a question of a scare my discovery on this occasion had scared me more than any other, and it was essentially in the scared state that I drew my actual conclusions. They harassed me so that sometimes, at odd moments, I shut myself up audibly to rehearse – it was at once a fantastic relief and a renewed despair – the manner in which I might come to the point. I approached it from one side and the other while, in my room, I flung myself about, but I always broke down in the monstrous utterance of names. As they died away on my lips I said to myself that I should indeed help them to represent something infamous if by pronouncing them I should violate as rare a little case of instinctive delicacy as any schoolroom probably had ever known. When I said to myself: '*they* have the manners to be silent, and you, trusted as you are, the baseness to speak!' I felt myself crimson and covered my face with my hands. After these secret scenes I chattered more than ever, going on volubly enough

consummation: result

in a proportionate…my pupils: thought that the children were aware of the ghosts

had I not been…have broken out: if talking about the ghosts would have done more good than harm then she would have brought the subject up

the mockery of their advantage: the writer is suggesting that the children know the Governess is afraid to talk about ghosts because it would sound so odd

utterance of names: saying the names of Quint and Miss Jessel

that I should…had ever known: by talking about the children she would make them evil and break the polite calm of the schoolroom

COMMENTARY

Still convinced that the children 'see' the ghosts, even when she is with them, the Governess considers bringing the subject up but is afraid of frightening Miles and Flora and appearing foolish.

till one of our prodigious palpable hushes occurred – I can call them nothing else – the strange dizzy lift or swim (I try for terms!) into a stillness, a pause of all life, that had nothing to do with the more or less noise we at the moment might be engaged in making and that I could hear through any intensified mirth or quickened recitation or louder strum of the piano. Then it was that the others, the outsiders, were there. Though they were not angels they 'passed', as the French say, causing me, while they stayed, to tremble with the fear of their addressing to their younger victims some yet more infernal message or more vivid image than they had thought good enough for myself.

What it was least possible to get rid of was the cruel idea that, whatever I had seen, Miles and Flora saw *more* – things terrible and unguessable and that sprang from dreadful passages of intercourse in the past. Such things naturally left on the surface, for the time, a chill that we vociferously denied we felt; and we had all three, with repetition, got into such splendid training that we went, each time, to mark the close of the incident, almost automatically through the very same movements. It was striking of the children at all events to kiss me inveterately with a wild irrelevance and never to fail – one or the other – of the precious question that had helped us through many a period. 'When do you think he *will* come? Don't you think we *ought* to write?' – there was nothing like that inquiry, we found by experience, for carrying off an awkwardness. 'He' of course was their uncle in Harley Street; and we lived in much profusion of theory that he might at any moment arrive to mingle in our circle. It was impossible to have given less encouragement than he had administered to such a doctrine, but if we had not had the doctrine to fall back upon we should have deprived each other of some of our finest exhibitions. He never wrote to them – that may have been selfish, but it was a part of the flattery of his trust of myself; for the way in which a man pays his highest tribute to a woman is apt to be but by the more festal celebration of one of the sacred laws of his comfort. So I held that I carried out the spirit of the pledge given not to appeal to him when I let our young friends understand that their own letters were but charming literary exercises. They were too beautiful to be posted; I

COMMENTARY

The Governess is aware when the ghosts are there, even though she cannot see them and is afraid of what they are saying to the children. She and the children talk about the uncle coming to see them. The children write to him but the Governess does not send the letters because this would break her promise never to disturb him.

prodigious palpable hushes: long and awkward silences
try for terms: struggle for words
into a stillness…strum of the piano: the children always made more noise when the ghosts were there
the outsiders: Quint and Miss Jessel
vociferously: in strong terms
inveterately: always
in much profusion of theory: with many ideas
to mingle in our circle: to be with us
than he had administered to such a doctrine: to this idea
apt to be…of his comfort: usually given when she makes his life more comfortable

kept them myself; I have them all to this hour. This was a rule indeed which only added to the satiric effect of my being plied with the supposition that he might at any moment be among us. It was exactly as if our young friends knew how almost more awkward than anything else that might be for me. There appears to me, moreover, as I look back no note in all this more extraordinary than the mere fact that, in spite of my tension and of their triumph, I never lost patience with them. Adorable they must in truth have been, I now feel, since I didn't in these days hate them! Would exasperation, however, if relief had longer been postponed, finally have betrayed me? It little matters, for relief arrived. I call it relief though it was only the relief that a snap brings to a strain or the burst of a thunderstorm to a day of suffocation.

▶▶ It was at least change, and it came with a rush.

REWIND: …came with a rush.

The Governess thinks that Miles and Flora are secretly enjoying her difficulty in finding out what is happening between the ghosts and the children. They ask lots of questions about the Governess's childhood and so are able to avoid the subject of Quint and Miss Jessel. The Governess has not seen the ghosts for some time and thinks that they are appearing only to the children; she feels frustrated that she cannot defend them against the influence of the ghosts.

They wonder when the children's uncle will come and see them. Miles and Flora write to him but the Governess does not send the letters.

---

satiric effect…supposition: humour arising from their thinking that
Would exasperation…betrayed me: the Governess wonders if she would have finally lost her patience if the situation had not changed

COMMENTARY
The children seem to realise how awkward a visit from the uncle would be for the Governess; not only would the story of the ghosts sound silly but she would have to explain why Miles was not at school.

Look out for...
- how we hear Miles's voice directly for the first time – is your opinion of him changed in any way?
- the Governess's attitude to Miles and his suggestions.

FAST FORWARD: to page 102

Walking to church a certain Sunday morning, I had little Miles at my side and his sister, in advance of us and at Mrs Grose's, well in sight. It was a crisp clear day, the first of its order for some time; the night had brought a touch of frost and the autumn air, bright and sharp, made the church-bells almost gay. It was an odd accident of thought that I should have happened at such a moment to be particularly and very gratefully struck with the obedience of my little charges. Why did they never resent my inexorable, my perpetual society? Something or other had brought nearer home to me that I had all but pinned the boy to my shawl, and that in the way our companions were marshalled before me I might have appeared to provide against some danger of rebellion. I was like a gaoler with an eye to possible surprises and escapes. But all this belonged – I mean their magnificent little surrender – just to the special

COMMENTARY
Walking to church one Sunday the Governess realises that, in her fear of the ghosts 'getting at' the children, she has become like a jailer and is always in their company.

gay: happy
my little charges: those in her care
inexorable, my perpetual society: constant company
marshalled: organised

array of the facts that were most abysmal. Turned out for Sunday by his uncle's tailor, who had had a free hand and a notion of pretty waistcoats and of his grand little air, Miles's whole title to independence, the rights of his sex and situation, were so stamped upon him that if he had suddenly struck for freedom I should have had nothing to say. I was by the strangest of chances wondering how I should meet him when the revolution unmistakably occurred. I call it a revolution because I now see how, with the word he spoke, the curtain rose on the last act of my dreadful drama and the catastrophe was precipitated. 'Look here, my dear, you know,' he charmingly said, 'when in the world, please, am I going back to school?'

Transcribed here the speech sounds harmless enough, particularly as uttered in the sweet, high, casual pipe with which, at all interlocutory, but above all at his eternal governess, he threw off intonations as if he were tossing roses. There was something in them that always made one 'catch', and I caught at any rate now so effectually that I stopped as short as if one of the trees of the park had fallen across the road. There was something new, on the spot, between us, and he was perfectly aware I recognised it, though to enable me to do so he had no need to look a whit less candid and charming than usual. I could feel in him how he already, from my at first finding nothing to reply, perceived the advantage he had gained. I was so slow to find anything that he had plenty of time, after a minute, to continue with his suggestive but inconclusive smile: 'You know, my dear, that for a fellow to be with a lady *always*—!' His 'my dear' was constantly on his lips for me, and nothing could have expressed more the exact shade of the sentiment with which I desired to

---

REWIND: …he had gained.
Going into church one Sunday, Miles has asked the Governess when he is going back to school. The Governess does not want to answer and Miles sees that he has an advantage over his teacher, who, he realises, does not want him to go away to school.

---

abysmal: terrible
the rights of his sex and situation: the writer is
    saying that Miles is rich and male and can
    therefore do what he wants
precipitated: brought on
at all interlocutory: to everyone he spoke to
catch: stop short
a whit less candid: one little bit less honest

COMMENTARY
As they walk, Miles asks the Governess when he is going to school. The Governess realises that this question has been overlooked for too long and that in mentioning it first, Miles has an advantage over her.

inspire my pupils than its fond familiarity. It was so respectfully easy.

But oh how I felt that at present I must pick my own phrases! I remember that, to gain time, I tried to laugh, and I seemed to see in the beautiful face with which he watched me how ugly and queer I looked. 'And always with the same lady?' I returned.

He neither blenched nor winked. The whole thing was virtually out between us. 'Ah of course she's a jolly "perfect" lady; but after all I'm a fellow, don't you see? who's – well, getting on.'

I lingered there with him an instant ever so kindly. 'Yes, you're getting on.' Oh but I felt helpless!

I have kept to this day the heartbreaking little idea of how he seemed to know that and to play with it. 'And you can't say I've not been awfully good, can you?'

I laid my hand on his shoulder, for though I felt how much better it would have been to walk on I was not yet quite able. 'No, I can't say that, Miles.'

'Except just that one night, you know—!'

'That one night?' I couldn't look as straight as he.

'Why, when I went down – went out of the house.'

'Oh yes. But I forget what you did it for.'

'You forget?' – he spoke with the sweet extravagance of childish reproach. 'Why, it was just to show you I could!'

'Oh yes – you could.'

'And I can again.'

I felt I might perhaps after all succeed in keeping my wits about me. 'Certainly. But you won't.'

'No, not *that* again. It was nothing.'

'It was nothing,' I said. 'But we must go on.'

He resumed our walk with me, passing his hand into my arm. 'Then when *am* I going back?'

I wore, in turning it over, my most responsible air. 'Were you very happy at school?'

COMMENTARY

Miles points out that he is getting older and needs more than a Governess. The Governess is nervous during this conversation because she knows that there are secrets between them about Miles's schooling; she has never told the uncle that he has been expelled and Miles has never told her why.

blenched: went white
sweet extravagance of childish reproach: exaggerated hurt

He just considered. 'Oh I'm happy enough anywhere!'

'Well, then,' I quavered, 'if you're just as happy here—!'

'Ah but that isn't everything! Of course *you* know a lot—'

'But you hint that you know almost as much?' I risked as he paused.

'Not half I want to!' Miles honestly professed. 'But it isn't so much that.'

'What is it, then?'

'Well – I want to see more life.'

'I see; I see.' We had arrived within sight of the church and of various persons, including several of the household of Bly, on their way to it and

clustered about the door to see us go in. I quickened our step; I wanted to get there before the question between us opened up much further; I reflected hungrily that he would have for more than a hour to be silent; and I thought with envy of the comparative dusk of the pew and of the almost spiritual help of the hassock on which I might bend my knees. I seemed literally to be running a race with some confusion to which he was about to reduce me, but I felt he had got in first when, before we had even entered the churchyard, he threw out:

'I want my own sort!'

It literally made me bound forward. 'There aren't many of your own sort, Miles!' I laughed. 'Unless perhaps dear little Flora!'

'You really compare me to a baby girl?'

opened up much further: continued

pew: bench seat

hassock: a prayer cushion

I seemed literally…to reduce me: she wants to get into the quiet of the church before Miles's words upset her too much

COMMENTARY

Miles continues to say that he wants to see more than just Bly and that he wants to be with other boys and men. The Governess does not want to talk about this subject because it is caught up in her mind with all the difficulties of her life; the ghosts, the headmaster's letter and her strong feelings for the uncle.

This found me singularly weak. 'Don't you, then, *love* our sweet Flora?'

'If I didn't – and you too; if I didn't—!' he repeated as if retreating for a jump, yet leaving his thought so unfinished that, after we had come into the gate, another stop, which he imposed on me by the pressure of his arm, had become inevitable. Mrs Grose and Flora had passed into the church, the other worshippers had followed and we were, for the minute, alone among the old thick graves. We had paused, on the path from the gate, by a low oblong table-like tomb.

'Yes, if you didn't—?'

He looked, while I waited, about at the graves. 'Well, you know what!' But he didn't move, and he presently produced something that made me drop straight down on the stone slab as if suddenly to rest. 'Does my uncle think what *you* think?'

I markedly rested. 'How do you know what I think?'

'Ah well, of course I don't; for it strikes me you never tell me. But I mean does *he* know?'

'Know what, Miles?'

'Why, the way I'm going on.'

I recognised quickly enough that I could make, to this inquiry, no answer that wouldn't involve something of a sacrifice of my employer. Yet it struck me that we were all, at Bly, sufficiently sacrificed to make that venial. 'I don't think your uncle much cares.'

Miles, on this, stood looking at me. 'Then don't you think he can be made to?'

'In what way?'

'Why, by his coming down.'

'But who'll get him to come down?'

'*I* will!' the boy said with extraordinary brightness and emphasis. He gave me another look charged with that expression and then marched off alone into church.

COMMENTARY

Alone now in the churchyard the others having gone in, Miles asks the Governess if his uncle knows that he has not gone back to school. She tells him that his uncle does not care whether he has or not. Miles says that he is going to get him to come down to Bly. He goes into the church leaving the Governess alone amongst the graves.

no answer that…my employer: her answer would mean telling Miles that his uncle did not wish to be bothered with them

venial: justifiable

15

Look out for...
- the Governess's reasons for not following the others into the church.
- what she now intends to do.
- the similarities between the Governess and Miss Jessel. What comparisons are there between them?

The business was practically settled from the moment I never followed him. It was a pitiful surrender to agitation, but my being aware of this had somehow no power to restore me. I only sat there on my tomb and read into what our young friend had said to me the fulness of its meaning; by the time I had grasped the whole of which I had also embraced, for absence, the pretext that I was ashamed to offer my pupils and the rest of the congregation such an example of delay. What I said to myself above all was that Miles had got something out of me and that the gage of it for him would be just this awkward collapse. He had got out of me that there was something I was much afraid of, and that he should probably be able to make use of my fear to gain, for his own purpose, more freedom. My fear was of having to deal with the intolerable question of the grounds of his dismissal from school, since that was really but the question of the horrors gathered behind. That his uncle should arrive to treat with me of these things was a solution that, strictly speaking, I ought now to have desired to bring on; but I could so little face the ugliness and the pain of it that I simply procrastinated and lived from hand to mouth.

surrender to agitation: giving in to being anxious

embraced, for absence, the pretext: gave herself as a reason for not going into church

the gage of it for him would be just this awkward collapse: he would see how much of an advantage he had by her length of delay in going into church

but the questions…behind: the questions about Quint and Miss Jessel

treat with me: deal with me

procrastinated: delayed

COMMENTARY

The Governess does not follow Miles into church. She realises that in asking to go to school Miles has touched on all her secret fears; why was he expelled? What is the connection between that and the ghosts? How will the uncle's opinion of her be changed if he comes to Bly? She feels that Miles will use his advantage to get more freedom.

The boy, to my deep discomposure, was immensely in the right, was in a position to say to me: 'Either you clear up with my guardian the mystery of this interruption of my studies, or you cease to expect me to lead with you a life that's so unnatural for a boy.' What was so unnatural for the particular boy I was concerned with was this sudden revelation of a consciousness and a plan.

That was what really overcame me, what prevented my going in. I walked round the church, hesitating, hovering; I reflected that I had already, with him, hurt myself beyond repair. Therefore I could patch up nothing and it was too extreme an effort to squeeze beside him into the pew: he would be so much more sure than ever to pass his arm into mine and make me sit there for a hour in close mute contact with his commentary on our talk. For the first minute since his arrival I wanted to get away from him. As I paused beneath the high cast window and listened to the sounds of worship I was taken with an impulse that might master me, I felt, and completely, should I give it the least encouragement. I might easily put an end to my ordeal by getting away altogether. Here was my chance; there was no one to stop me; I could give the whole thing up – turn my back and bolt. It was only a question of hurrying again, for a few preparations, to the house which the attendance at church of so many of the servants would practically have left unoccupied. No one, in short, could blame me if I should just drive desperately off. What was it to get away if I should get away only till dinner? That would be in a couple of hours, at the end of which – I had the acute prevision – my little pupils would play at innocent wonder about my non-appearance in their train.

'What *did* you do, you naughty bad thing? Why in the world, to worry us so – and take our thoughts off too, don't you know? – did you desert us at the very door?' I couldn't meet such questions nor, as they asked them, their false little lovely eyes; yet it was all so exactly what I should have to meet that, as the prospect grew sharp to me, I at last let myself go.

I got, so far as the immediate moment was concerned, away; I came straight out of the churchyard and, thinking hard, retraced my steps through the park. It seemed to me that by the time I reached the house I had made up my mind

COMMENTARY
The Governess is shocked by what she sees as Miles's plan to blackmail her into giving him more freedom at Bly by threatening to bring the uncle to Bly so that she would have to explain herself to him. She dreads having to explain to the children why she did not follow them into church. To avoid all these problems she decides to leave Bly and returns to the house with this purpose in mind.

discomposure: discomfort
my guardian: Miles's uncle
revelation…and a plan: realisation that he had a plan
mute: silent
acute prevision: clearly saw into the future
train: group

to cynical flight. The Sunday stillness both of the approaches and of the interior, in which I met no one, fairly stirred me with a sense of opportunity. Were I to get off quickly this way I should get off without a scene, without a word. My quickness would have to be remarkable, however, and the question of a conveyance was the great one to settle. Tormented, in the hall, with difficulties and obstacles, I remember sinking down at the foot of the staircase – suddenly collapsing there on the lowest step and then, with a revulsion, recalling that it was exactly where, more than a month before, in the darkness of night and just so bowed with evil things, I had seen the spectre of the most horrible of women. At this I was able to straighten myself; I went the rest of the way up; I made, in my turmoil, for the schoolroom, where there were objects belonging to me that I should have to take. But I opened the door to find again, in a flash, my eyes unsealed. In the presence of what I saw I reeled straight back upon resistance.

Seated at my own table in the clear noonday light I saw a person whom, without my previous experience, I should have taken at the first blush for some housemaid who might have stayed at home to look after the place and who, availing herself of rare relief from observation and of the schoolroom table and my pens, ink and paper, had applied herself to the considerable effort of a letter to her sweetheart. There was an effort in the way that, while her arms rested on the table, her hands, with evident weariness, supported her head; but at the moment I took this in I had already become aware that, in spite of my entrance, her attitude strangely persisted. Then it was – with the very act of its announcing itself – that her identity flared up in a change of posture. She rose, not as if she had heard me, but with an indescribable grand melancholy of indifference and detachment, and, within a dozen feet of me, stood there as my vile predecessor. Dishonoured and tragic, she was all before me; but even as I fixed and, for memory, secured it, the awful image passed away. Dark as midnight in her black dress, her haggard beauty and her unutterable woe, she had looked at me long enough to appear to say that her right to sit at my table was as good as mine to sit at hers. While these instants

cynical flight: selfish departure
conveyance: carriage
bowed: troubled
spectre: ghost
unsealed: were able to see ghosts
first blush: first sight
availing herself of rare relief: taking advantage of a rare privacy
vile predecessor: Miss Jessel

COMMENTARY
Once in the house, the Governess pauses on the stairs and sits down, worn out by her worries. She realises that she is sitting in the same position that she had seen Miss Jessel one night. She goes to the schoolroom to collect some of her things and, as she enters, she sees someone sitting at her desk. When the figure gets up the Governess realises that she is looking at Miss Jessel.

lasted indeed I had the extraordinary chill of a feeling that it was I who was the intruder. It was as a wild protest against it that, actually addressing her – 'You terrible miserable woman!' – I heard myself break into a sound that, by the open door, rang through the long passage and the empty house. She looked at me as if she heard me, but I had recovered myself and cleared the air. There was nothing in the room the next minute but the sunshine and the sense that I must stay.

COMMENTARY

Miss Jessel disappears when the Governess speaks to her. However, her ability to see the ghosts again has made the Governess change her mind. She is now determined to stay at Bly and fight the ghosts for control of the children.

16

Look out for...
- **the reason why nobody asks the Governess why she has not gone into church.**
- **the conclusion that Mrs Grose and the Governess come to about why Miles has been expelled.**

I had so perfectly expected the return of the others to be marked by a demonstration that I was freshly upset at having to find them merely dumb and discreet about my desertion. Instead of *gaily denouncing and caressing me* they made no allusion to my having failed them, and I was left, for the time, on perceiving that she too said nothing, to study Mrs Grose's odd face. I did this to such purpose that I made sure they had in some way bribed her to silence; a silence that, however, I would engage to break down on the first private opportunity. This opportunity came before tea: I secured five minutes with her in the housekeeper's room, where, in the twilight, amid a smell of lately-baked bread, but with the place all swept and *garnished*, I found her sitting in pained *placidity* before the fire. So I see her still, so I see her best: facing the flame from her straight chair in the dusky shining room, a large clean picture of the 'put away' – of drawers closed and locked and *rest without a remedy*.

'Oh yes, they asked me to say nothing; and to please them – so long as they were there – of course I promised. But what had happened to you?'

COMMENTARY
To the Governess's surprise, the children and Mrs Grose do not ask her why she did not follow them into church.
When she is alone with Mrs Grose the Governess questions her about this.

gaily denouncing and caressing me: making friendly fun of her failure to go to church
garnished: cleaned
placidity: stillness
rest without a remedy: everything organised

'I only went with you for the walk,' I said. 'I had then to come back to meet a friend.'

She showed her surprise. 'A friend – *you?*'

'Oh yes, I've a couple!' I laughed. 'But did the children give you a reason?'

'For not alluding to your leaving us?' Yes; they said you'd like it better. *Do you like it better?*'

My face had made her rueful. 'No, I like it worse!' But after an instant added: 'Did they say why I should like it better?'

'No; Master Miles only said "We must do nothing but what she likes!"'

'I wish indeed he would! And what did Flora say?'

'Miss Flora was too sweet. She said "Oh of course, of course!" – and I said the same.'

I thought a moment. 'You were too sweet too – I can hear you all. But none the less, between Miles and me, it's now all out.'

'All out?' My companion stared. 'But what, Miss?'

'Everything. It doesn't matter. I've made up my mind. I came home, my dear,' I went on, 'for a talk with Miss Jessel.'

I had by this time formed the habit of having Mrs Grose literally well in hand in advance of my sounding that note; so that even now, as she bravely blinked under the signal of my word, I could keep her comparatively firm. 'A talk! Do you mean she spoke?'

'It came to that. I found her, on my return, in the schoolroom.'

'And what did she say?' I can hear the good woman still, and the candour of her stupefaction.

'That she suffers the torments—!'

It was this, of a truth, that made her, as she filled out my picture, gape. 'Do you mean,' she faltered '—of the lost?'

'Of the lost. Of the damned. And that's why, to share them—' I faltered myself with the horror of it.

But my companion, with less imagination, kept me up. 'To share them—?'

'She wants Flora.' Mrs Grose might, as I gave it to her, fairly have fallen away from me had I not been prepared. I still held her there, to show I was. 'As I've told you, however, it doesn't matter.'

'Because you've made up your mind? But to what?'

'To everything.'

'And what do you call "everything"?'

'Why, to sending for their uncle.'

'Oh Miss, in pity do,' my friend broke out.

'Ah but I will, I *will*! I see it's the only way. What's "out", as I told you, with Miles is that if he thinks I'm afraid to – and has ideas of what he gains by that – he shall see he's mistaken. Yes, yes; his uncle shall have it here from me on the spot (and before the boy himself if necessary) that if I'm to be reproached with having done nothing again about more school—'

'Yes, Miss—' my companion pressed me.

'Well, there's that awful reason.'

There were now clearly so many of these for my poor colleague that she was excusable for being vague. 'But – a – which?'

'Why, the letter from his old place.'

'You'll show it to the master?'

'I ought to have done so on the instant.'

'Oh no!' said Mrs Grose with decision.

'I'll put it before him,' I went on inexorably, 'that I can't undertake to work the question on behalf of a child who has been expelled—'

'For we've never in the least known what!' Mrs Grose declared.

'For wickedness. For what else – when he's so clever and beautiful and perfect? Is he stupid? Is he untidy? Is he infirm? Is he ill-natured? He's exquisite – so it can be only *that*; and that would open up the whole thing. After all,' I said, 'it's their uncle's fault. If he left here such people—!'

'He didn't really in the least know them. The fault's mine.' She had turned quite pale.

'Well, you shan't suffer,' I answered.

'The children shan't!' she emphatically returned.

---

reproached: blamed
inexorably: firmly

COMMENTARY
The Governess now thinks that Miles must have been expelled for being 'wicked' and blames the uncle for leaving the children in the hands of Quint. She decides that the only solution is to send for the uncle to visit Bly and to show him the headmaster's letter.

I was silent a while; we looked at each other. 'Then what am I to tell him?'

'You needn't tell him anything. *I'll* tell him.'

I measured this. 'Do you mean you'll write—?' Remembering she couldn't, I caught myself up. 'How do you communicate?'

'I tell the bailiff. *He* writes.'

'And should you like him to write our story?'

My question had a sarcastic force that I had not fully intended, and it made her after a moment inconsequently break down. The tears were again in her eyes. 'Ah Miss, *you* write!'

'Well – to-night,' I at last returned; and on this we separated.

COMMENTARY

The Governess tells Mrs Grose that she will write to the uncle and ask him to come to Bly.

bailiff: the estate manager
inconsequently: without reason

17

Look out for...
● **Henry James's descriptions of the sleeping house. Why is this important to the events in the chapter?**
● **the Governess's attempts to get Miles to tell her all about his school and the ghosts.**

I went so far, in the evening, as to make a beginning. The weather had changed back, a great wind was abroad, and beneath the lamp, in my room, with Flora at peace beside me, I sat for a long time before a blank sheet of paper and listened to the lash of the rain and the batter of the gusts. Finally I went out, taking a candle; I crossed the passage and listened a minute at Miles's door. What, under my endless obsession, I had been impelled to listen for was some betrayal of his not being at rest, and I presently caught one, but not in the form I had expected. His voice tinkled out. 'I say, you there – come in.' It was gaiety in the gloom!

I went in with my light and found him in bed, very wide awake but very much as his ease. 'Well, what are *you* up to?' he asked with a grace of sociability in which it occurred to me that Mrs Grose, had she been present, might have looked in vain for proof that anything was 'out'.

I stood over him with my candle. 'How did you know I was there?'

'Why of course I heard you. Did you fancy you made no noise? You're like a troop of cavalry!' he beautifully laughed.

impelled: forced
grace of sociability: confidence
Mrs Grose...was out: the Governess has said to Mrs Grose that they had no secrets between them

COMMENTARY
That night, unable to finish her letter to the uncle, the Governess leaves her room and listens at Miles's door to make sure that he is asleep. Miles hears her and calls her into his room.

'Then you weren't asleep?'

'Not much! I lie awake and think.'

I had put my candle, designedly, a short way off, and then, as he held out his friendly old hand to me, had sat down on the edge of his bed. 'What is it,' I asked, 'that you think of?'

'What in the world, my dear, but *you?*'

'Ah, the pride I take in your appreciation doesn't insist on that! I had so far rather you slept.'

'Well, I think also, you know, of this queer business of ours.'

I marked the coolness of his firm little hand. 'Of what queer business, Miles?'

'Why, the way you bring me up. And all the rest!'

I fairly held my breath in minute, and even from my glimmering taper there was light enough to show how he smiled up at me from his pillow. 'What do you mean by all the rest?'

'Oh you know, you know!'

I could say nothing for a minute, though I felt as I held his hand and our eyes continued to meet that my silence had all the air of admitting his charge and that nothing in the whole world of reality was perhaps at that moment so fabulous as our actual relation. 'Certainly you shall go back to school,' I said, 'if it be that that troubles you. But not to the old place – we must find another, a better. How could I know it did trouble you, this question, when you never told me so, never spoke of it at all?' His clear listening face, framed in its smooth whiteness, made him for the minute as appealing as some wistful patient in a children's hospital; and I would have given, as the resemblance came to me, all I possessed on earth really to be the nurse or the sister of charity who might have helped to cure him. Well, even as it was I perhaps might help! 'Do you know you've never said a word to me about your school – I mean the old one; never mentioned it in any way?'

He seemed to wonder; he smiled with the same loveliness. But he clearly gained time; he waited, he called for guidance. 'Haven't I?' It wasn't for *me* to help him – it was for the thing I had met!

COMMENTARY

Miles tells the Governess that he lies awake at night thinking about going back to school. This surprises the Governess who reminds him that he has never talked about school to her.

Ah, the pride…on that: the Governess is saying that he need not flatter her, even though she is proud to be in his thoughts

fabulous: unreal

wistful: thoughtful

It wasn't for me…I had met: if Miles was to get any help in explaining the situation then the Governess feels it should be from Quint and not her

Something in his tone and the expression of his face, as I got this from him, set my heart aching with such a pang as it had never yet known; so unutterably touching was it to see his little brain puzzled and his little resources taxed to play, under the spell laid on him, a part of innocence and consistency. 'No, never – from the hour you came back. You've never mentioned to me one of your masters, one of your comrades, nor the least little thing that ever happened to you at school. Never, little Miles – no, never – have you given me an inkling of anything that *may* have happened there. Therefore you can fancy how much I'm in the dark. Until you came out, that way, this morning, you had since the first hour I saw you scarce even made a reference to anything in your previous life. You seemed so perfectly to accept the present.' It was extraordinary how my absolute conviction of his secret precocity – or whatever I might call the poison of an influence that I dared but half-phrase – made him, in spite of the faint breath of his inward trouble, appear as accessible as an older person, forced me to treat him as an intelligent equal. 'I thought you wanted to go on as you are.'

It struck me that at this he just faintly coloured. He gave, at any rate, like a convalescent slightly fatigued, a languid shake of his head. 'I don't – I don't. I want to get away.'

'You're tired of Bly?'

'Oh no, I like Bly.'

'Well then—?'

'Oh *you* know what a boy wants!'

I felt I didn't know so well as Miles, and I took temporary refuge. 'You want to go to your uncle?'

Again, at this, with his sweet ironic face, he made a movement on the pillow. 'Ah you can't get off with that!'

I was silent a little, and it was I now, I think, who changed colour. 'My dear, I don't want to get off!'

'You can't even if you do. You can't, you can't!' – he lay beautifully staring. 'My uncle must come down and you must completely settle things.'

---

his little resources…and consistency: it was hard for him to play the innocent while he is being told what to do by Quint

inkling: idea

his secret precocity…intelligent equal: the Governess thinks that he has the understanding and maturity of a much older person and, far from being an innocent child, he is being directly told what to do and say by the ghost of Quint. Because of this she treats him like an adult and not a boy

COMMENTARY
Miles denies the Governess's challenge to him that he wanted to stay at Bly. He insists that the Governess makes the uncle come to Bly to sort out a new school for him.

'If we do,' I returned with some spirit, 'you may be sure it will be to take you quite away.'

'Well, don't you understand that that's exactly what I'm working for? You'll have to *tell* him – about the way you've let it all drop: you'll have to tell him a tremendous lot!'

The exultation with which he uttered this helped me somehow for the instant to meet him rather more. 'And how much will *you*, Miles, have to tell him? There are things he'll ask you!'

He turned it over. 'Very likely. But what things?'

'The things you've never told me. To make up his mind what to do with you. He can't send you back—'

'I don't want to go back!' he broke in. 'I want a new field.'

He said it with admirable serenity, with positive unimpeachable gaiety; and doubtless it was that very note that most evoked for me the poignancy, the unnatural childish tragedy, of his probable reappearance at the end of three months with all this bravado and still more dishonour. It overwhelmed me now that I should never be able to bear that, and it made me let myself go. I threw myself upon him and in the tenderness of my pity I embraced him. 'Dear little Miles, dear little Miles—!'

My face was close to his, and he let me kiss him, simply taking it with indulgent good humour. 'Well, old lady?'

'Is there nothing – nothing at all that you want to tell me?'

He turned off a little, facing round toward the wall and holding up his hand to look at as one had seen sick children look. 'I've told you – I told you this morning.'

Oh I was sorry for him! 'That you just want me not to worry you?'

He looked round at me now as if in recognition of my understanding him; then ever so gently, 'To let me alone,' he replied.

There was even a strange little dignity in it, something that made me release him, yet, when I had slowly risen, linger beside him. God knows *I* never wished to harass him, but I felt that merely, at this, to turn my back on him

---

COMMENTARY

Miles and the Governess realise that if the uncle comes to Bly then they will both have some explaining to do. Miles says that he just wants more freedom at Bly, and that if the Governess allows this then the uncle need not be brought down and she will be spared from explaining why she did not tell him about the headmaster's letter. What Miles did at school can also remain a secret.

exultation: triumph
serenity: calm
unimpeachable gaiety: unspoilt happiness
evoked: made clear
his probable reappearance…more dishonour: after another term Miles would return with more evil acts on his record but equally casual about them

was to abandon or, to put it more truly, lose him. 'I've just begun a letter to your uncle,' I said.

'Well then, finish it!'

I waited a minute. 'What happened before?'

He gazed up at me again. 'Before what?'

'Before you came back. And before you went away.'

For some time he was silent, but he continued to meet my eyes. 'What happened?'

It made me, the sound of the words, in which it seemed to me I caught for the very first time a small faint quaver of consenting consciousness – it made me drop on my knees beside the bed and seize once more the chance of possessing him. 'Dear little Miles, dear little Miles, if you *knew* how I want to help you! It's only that, it's nothing but that, and I'd rather die than give you a pain or do you a wrong – I'd rather die than hurt a hair of you. Dear little Miles' – oh I brought it out now even if I *should* go too far – 'I just want you to help me to save you!' But I knew in a moment after this that I had gone too far. The answer to my appeal was instantaneous, but it came in the form of an extraordinary blast and chill, a gust of frozen air and a shake of the room as great as if, in the wild wind, the casement had crashed in. The boy gave a loud high shriek which, lost in the rest of the shock of sound, might have seemed, indistinctly, though I was so close to him, a note either of jubilation or of terror. I jumped to my feet again and was conscious of darkness. So for a moment we remained, while I stared about me and saw the drawn curtains unstirred and window still tight. 'Why, the candle's out!' I then cried.

'It was I who blew it, dear!' said Miles.

a small faint quaver...consciousness:
  a hint that he is about to tell
  her everything
instantaneous: immediate
casement: window
jubilation: joy

COMMENTARY
The Governess finally asks Miles what he did at school and what happened at Bly the previous summer. She also tells him that she wants to save him from Quint's influence. Miles responds by screaming loudly and blowing out the candle.

FAST FORWARD: to page 122

The next day, after lessons, Mrs Grose found a moment to say to me quietly: 'Have you written, Miss?'

'Yes – I've written,' But I didn't add – for the hour – that my letter, sealed and directed, was still in my pocket. There would be time enough to send it before the messenger should go to the village. Meanwhile there had been on the part of my pupils no more brilliant, more exemplary morning. It was exactly as if they had both had at heart to gloss over any recent little friction. They performed the dizziest feats of arithmetic, soaring quite out of *my* feeble range, and perpetrated, in higher spirits than ever, geographical and historical jokes. It was conspicuous of course in Miles in particular that he appeared to wish to show how easily he could let me down. This child, to my memory, really lives in a setting of beauty and misery that no words can translate;

COMMENTARY
The Governess completes the letter to the children's uncle but does not send it. Miles and Flora continue to be model pupils

exemplary: faultless
friction: argument
perpetrated: made
conspicuous: obvious

there was a distinction all his own in every impulse he revealed; never was a small natural creature, to the uninformed eye all frankness and freedom, a more ingenious, a more extraordinary little gentleman. I had perpetually to guard against the wonder of contemplation into which my initiated view betrayed me; to check the irrelevant gaze and discouraged sigh in which I constantly both attacked and renounced the enigma of what such a little gentleman could have done that deserved a penalty. Say that, by the dark prodigy I knew, the imagination of all evil *had* been opened up to him: all the justice within me ached for the proof that it could ever have flowered into an act.

He had never at any rate been such a little gentleman as when, after our early dinner on this dreadful day, he came round to me and asked if I shouldn't like him for half an hour to play to me. David playing to Saul could never have shown a finer sense of the occasion. It was literally a charming exhibition of tact, of magnanimity, and quite tantamount to his saying outright: 'The true knights we love to read about never push an advantage too far. I know what you mean now: you mean that – to be let alone yourself and not followed up – you'll cease to worry and spy upon me, won't keep me so close to you, will let me go and come. Well, I "come", you see – but I don't go! There'll be plenty of time for that. I do really delight in your society and I only want to show you that I contended for a principle.' It may be imagined whether I resisted this appeal or failed to accompany him again, hand in hand, to the schoolroom. He sat down at the old piano and played as he had never played; and if there are those who think he had better have been kicking a football I can only say that I wholly agree with them. For at the end of a time that under his influence I had quite ceased to measure I started up with a strange sense of having literally slept at my post. It was after luncheon, and by the schoolroom fire, and yet I hadn't really in the least slept; I had only done something much worse – I had forgotten. Where all this time was Flora? When I put the question to Miles he played on a minute before answering, and then could only say: 'Why, my dear, how do *I* know?' – breaking, moreover, into a

---

I had perpetually…deserved a penalty: she had to be careful not to believe that Miles deserved to be expelled

the dark prodigy: Quint

David playing to Saul: a reference to the Bible story in which David played soothing harp music to King Saul

magnanimity: generosity

tantamount: amounted to

contended: argued

COMMENTARY
Even though Miles was exposed to evil, the Governess cannot believe that he was actually wicked. Miles plays the piano for the Governess to show her that he is not going to ignore her even though he has more freedom.

happy laugh which immediately after, as if it were a vocal accompaniment, he prolonged into incoherent extravagant song.

I went straight to my room, but his sister was not there; then, before going downstairs, I looked into several others. As she was nowhere about she would surely be with Mrs Grose, whom in the comfort of that theory I accordingly proceeded in quest of. I found her where I had found her the evening before, but she met my quick challenge with blank scared ignorance. She had only supposed that, after the repast, I had carried off both the children; as to which she was quite in her right, for it was the very first time I had allowed the little girl out of my sight without some special provision. Of course now indeed she might be with the maids, so that the immediate thing was to look for her without an air of alarm. This we promptly arranged between us; but when, ten minutes later and in pursuance of our arrangement, we met in the hall, it was only to report on either side that after guarded inquiries we had altogether failed to trace her. For a minute there, apart from observation, we

COMMENTARY

While Miles plays the piano the Governess forgets about Flora and what she might be doing. She suddenly becomes aware that she does not know where Flora is and, with Mrs Grose, she goes to look for her.

incoherent extravagant song: noisy nonsense
in quest of: to look for
repast: meal
in pursuance of: following

exchanged mute alarms, and I could feel with what high interest my friend
▶▶ returned me all those I had from the first given her.

'She'll be above,' she presently said – 'in one of the rooms you haven't
searched.'

'No; she's at a distance.' I had made up my mind. 'She has gone out.'

Mrs Grose stared. 'Without a hat?'

I naturally also looked volumes. 'Isn't that woman always without one?'

'She's with *her*?'

'She's with *her*!' I declared. 'We must find them.'

My hand was on my friend's arm, but she failed for the moment,
confronted with such an account of the matter, to respond to my pressure. She
communed, on the contrary, where she stood, with her uneasiness.

'And where's Master Miles?'

'Oh *he's* with Quint. They'll be in the schoolroom.'

'Lord, Miss!' My view, I was myself aware – and therefore I suppose my
tone – had never yet reached so calm an assurance.

'The trick's played,' I went on; 'they've successfully worked their plan. He
found the most divine little way to keep me quiet while she went off.'

'"Divine"?' Mrs Grose bewilderedly echoed.

'Infernal, then!' I almost cheerfully rejoined. 'He has provided for himself
as well. But come!'

She had helplessly gloomed at the upper regions. 'You leave him—?'

REWIND: …first given her.

The Governess tells Mrs Grose that she has written to the children's
uncle but does not tell her that she has not posted the letter yet. Miles
has played the piano to the Governess and she has been so charmed by his playing
that she has forgotten all about Flora. The Governess realises that Flora has
disappeared and cannot find her, either with Mrs Grose or the servants. Mrs Grose
is concerned.

---

exchanged mute alarms: gave
  each other a look in which
  they were able to share their
  anxieties without saying
  anything
looked volumes: gave her a
  meaningful look
She communed…her uneasiness:
  felt uneasy about the situation
divine: sweet and innocent
Infernal: devilish

COMMENTARY
The Governess thinks that Miles only played the
piano in order for Flora to slip away to Miss
Jessel and that Miles is now with Quint.

'So long with Quint? Yes – I don't mind that now.'

She always ended at these moments by getting possession of my hand, and in this manner she could at present still stay me. But after gasping an instant at my sudden resignation, 'Because of your letter?' she eagerly brought out.

I quickly, by way of answer, felt for my letter, drew it forth, held it up, and then, freeing myself, went and laid it on the great hall table. 'Luke will take it,' I said as I came back. I reached the house-door and opened it; I was already on the steps.

My companion still demurred: the storm of the night and the early morning had dropped, but the afternoon was damp and grey. I came down to the drive while she stood in the doorway. 'You go with nothing on?'

'What do I care when the child has nothing? I can't wait to dress,' I cried, 'and if you must do so I leave you. Try meanwhile yourself upstairs.'

'With *them*?' Oh on this the poor woman promptly joined me!

COMMENTARY
The Governess puts the letter to the children's uncle on the hall tray for posting and goes out of the house in search of Flora with Mrs Grose following her.

resignation: acceptance
demurred: hesitated

19

Look out for...
- **the way in which the Governess seems to be enjoying the situation in this chapter. How does Henry James bring this out?**
- **Flora's attitude when she is found by the lake.**

FAST FORWARD: to page 126

We went straight to the lake, as it was called at Bly, and I daresay rightly called, though it may have been a sheet of water less remarkable than my untravelled eyes supposed it. My acquaintance with sheets of water was small, and the pool of Bly, at all events on the few occasions of my consenting, under the protection of my pupils, to affront its surface in the old flat-bottomed board moored there for our use, had impressed me both with its extent and its agitation. The usual place of embarkation was half a mile from the house, but I had an intimate conviction that, wherever Flora might be, she was not near home. She had not given me the slip for any small adventure, and, since the day of the very great one that I had shared with her by the pond, I had been aware, in our walks, of the quarter to which she most

affront: disturb
extent: size
agitation: rough
  surface

COMMENTARY
The Governess and Mrs Grose go to the lake to look for Flora. Since the day Miss Jessel appeared there the Governess has noticed that Flora likes to play near the lake.

inclined. This was why I had now given to Mrs Grose's steps so marked a direction – a direction making her, when she perceived it, oppose a resistance that showed me she was freshly mystified. 'You're going to the water, Miss? – you think she's *in*—?'

'She may be, though the depth is, I believe, nowhere very great. But what I judge most likely is that she's on the spot from which, the other day, we saw together what I told you.'

'When she pretended not to see—?'

'With that astounding self-possession! I've always been sure she wanted to go back alone. And now her brother has managed it for her.'

Mrs Grose still stood where she had stopped. 'You suppose they really *talk* of them?'

I could meet this with an assurance! 'They say things that, if we heard them, would simply appal us.'

'And if she *is* there—?'

'Yes?'

'Then Miss Jessel is?'

'Beyond a doubt. You shall see.'

'Oh thank you!' my friend cried, planted so firm that, taking it in, I went straight on without her. By the time I reached the pool, however, she was close behind me, and I knew that, whatever, to her apprehension, might befall me, the exposure of sticking to me struck her as her least danger. She exhaled a moan of relief as we at last came in sight of the greater part of the water without a sight of the child. There was no trace of Flora on that nearer side of the bank where my observation of her had been most startling, and none on the opposite edge, where, save for a margin of some twenty yards, a thick copse came down to the pond. This expanse, oblong in shape, was so narrowed compared to its length that, with its ends out of view, it might have been taken for a scant river. We looked at the empty stretch, and then I felt the suggestion in my friend's eyes. I knew what she meant and I replied with a negative headshake.

COMMENTARY
The Governess and Mrs Grose return to the spot from where the Governess saw Miss Jessel, but there is no sign of Flora.

assurance: agreement
exhaled: let out
copse: wood

▶▶   'No, no; wait! She has taken the boat.'

My companion stared at the vacant mooring-place and then again across the lake. 'Then where is it?'

'Our not seeing it is the strongest of proofs. She has used it to go over, and then has managed to hide it.'

'All alone – that child?'

'She's not alone, and at such times she's not a child: she's an old, old woman.' I scanned all the visible shore while Mrs Grose took again, into the queer element I offered her, one of her plunges of submission; then I pointed out that the boat might perfectly be in a small refuge formed by one of the recesses of the pool, an indentation masked, for the hither side, by a projection of the bank and by a clump of trees growing close to the water.

'But if the boat's there, where on earth's *she*?' my colleague anxiously asked.

'That's exactly what we must learn.' And I started to walk further.

'By going all the way round?'

'Certainly, far as it is. It will take us but ten minutes, yet it's far enough to have made the child prefer not to walk. She went straight over.'

'Laws!' cried my friend again: the chain of my logic was ever too strong for her. It dragged her at my heels even now, and when we had got halfway round – a devious tiresome process, on ground much broken and by a path choked with overgrowth – I paused to give her breath. I sustained her with a grateful arm, assuring her that she might hugely help me; and this started us afresh, so that in the course of but few minutes more we reached a point from which we found the boat to be where I had supposed it. It had been intentionally left as

---

REWIND: …taken the boat.'
The Governess and Mrs Grose have gone to the lake in search of Flora.
The Governess thinks that the little girl has gone to meet Miss Jessel
and they discover that she has taken a rowing-boat across the water for this
purpose.   ◀◀ ◀

---

queer element: strange interpretation of
   events
indentation: inlet
the chain of my logic was ever too strong for her:
   she thinks that her understanding of the
   situation was always ahead of Mrs Grose's
a devious tiresome process: a roundabout route

COMMENTARY
The Governess and Mrs Grose notice that the boat which is usually by the lake shore has gone and they think that Flora has taken it to meet Miss Jessel on the other side of the lake. They begin to walk around the lake.

much as possible out of sight and was tied to one of the stakes of a fence that came, just there, down to the brink and that had been an assistance to disembarking. I recognised, as I looked at the pair of short thick oars, quite safely drawn up, the prodigious character of the feat for a little girl; but I had by this time lived too long among wonders and had panted to too many livelier measures. There was a gate in the fence, through which we passed, and that brought us after a trifling interval more into the open. Then 'There she is!' we both exclaimed at once.

Flora, a short way off, stood before us on the grass and smiled as if her performance had now become complete. The next thing she did, however, was to stoop straight down and pluck – quite as if it were all she was there for – a big ugly spray of withered fern. I at once felt sure she had just come out of the copse. She waited for us, not herself taking a step, and I was conscious of the rare solemnity with which we presently approached her. She smiled and smiled, and we met; but it was all done in a silence by this time flagrantly ominous. Mrs Grose was the first to break the spell: she threw herself on her knees and, drawing the child to her breast, clasped in a long embrace the little tender yielding body. While this dumb convulsion lasted I could only watch it – which I did the more intently when I saw Flora's face peep at me over our companion's shoulder. It was serious now – the flicker had left it; but it strengthened the pang with which I at that moment envied Mrs Grose the simplicity of *her* relation. Still, all this while, nothing more passed between us

save that Flora had let her foolish fern again drop to the ground. What she and I had virtually said to each other was that pretexts were useless now. When Mrs Grose finally got up she kept the child's hand, so that the two were still before me; and the singular reticence of our communion was even more marked in the frank look she addressed me. 'I'll be hanged,' it said, 'if *I'll* speak!'

It was Flora who, gazing all over me in candid wonder, was the first. She was struck with our bare-headed aspect. 'Why, where are your things?'

'Where yours are, my dear!' I promptly returned.

She had already got back her gaiety and appeared to take this as an answer quite sufficient. 'And where's Miles?' she went on.

There was something in the small valour of it that quite finished me: these three words from her were in a flash like the glitter of a drawn blade the jostle of the cup that my hand for weeks and weeks had held high and full to the brim and that now, even before speaking, I felt overflow in a deluge. 'I'll tell you if you'll tell *me*—' I heard myself say, then heard the tremor in which it broke.

'Well, what?'

Mrs Grose's suspense blazed at me, but it was too late now, and I brought the thing out handsomely. 'Where, my pet, is Miss Jessel?'

said to each other…useless now: the look between them meant that they could no longer hide the truth from each other

singular reticence: odd shyness

valour: courage

these three words from her…I felt overflow in a deluge: Flora's question has had the effect of bringing everything that has happened at Bly to a crisis point and making the Governess feel that she can no longer go on avoiding the truth with the children

Mrs Grose's suspense blazed at me: the writer is hinting that Mrs Grose does not want the Governess to ask Flora about Miss Jessel

COMMENTARY

Flora smiles at the Governess and Mrs Grose and asks where Miles is. The Governess is amazed at this question and replies by asking her where Miss Jessel is.

20

Look out for...
● the Governess's changed attitude to Flora.

FAST FORWARD: to page 131

J ust as in the churchyard with Miles, the whole thing was upon us. Much as I had made of the fact that this name had never once, between us, been sounded, the quick smitten glare with which the child's face now received it fairly likened my breach of the silence to the smash of a pane of glass. It added to the interposing cry, as if to stay the blow, that Mrs Grose at the same instant uttered over my violence – the shriek of a creature scared, or rather wounded, which, in turn, within a few seconds, was completed by a gasp of my own. I seized my colleague's arm. 'She's there, she's there!'

Miss Jessel stood before us on the opposite bank exactly as she had stood the other time, and I remember, strangely, as the first feeling now

COMMENTARY
Flora gives the Governess a shocked look and Mrs Grose cries out at the mention of the dead governess's name. At the same time the Governess sees Miss Jessel standing on the other side of the lake.

smitten: hurt
breach: breaking

produced in me, my thrill of joy at having brought on a proof. She was there, so I was justified; she was there, so I was neither cruel nor mad. She was there for poor scared Mrs Grose, but she was there most for Flora; and no moment of my monstrous time as perhaps so extraordinary as that in which I consciously threw out to her – with the sense that, pale and ravenous demon as she was, she would catch and understand it – an inarticulate message of gratitude. She rose erect on the spot my friend and I had lately quitted, and there wasn't in all the long reach of her desire an inch of her evil that fell short. This first vividness of vision and emotion were things of a few seconds, during which Mrs Grose's dazed blink across to where I pointed struck me as showing that she too at last saw, just as it carried my own eyes precipitately to the child. The revelation then of the manner in which Flora was affected startled me in truth far more than it would have done to find her also merely agitated, for direct dismay was of course not what I had expected. Prepared and on her guard as our pursuit had actually made her, she would repress every betrayal; and I was therefore at once shaken by my first glimpse of the particular one for which I had not allowed. To see her, without a convulsion of her small pink face, not even feign to glance in the direction of the prodigy I announced, but only, instead of that, turn at *me* an expression of hard still gravity, an expression absolutely new and unprecedented and that appeared to read and accuse and judge me – this was a stroke that somehow converted the little girl herself into a figure portentous. I gaped at her coolness even though my certitude of her thoroughly seeing was never greater than at that instant, and then, in the immediate need to defend myself, I called her passionately to witness. 'She's there, you little unhappy thing – there, there, *there*, and you know it as well as you know me!' I had said shortly before to Mrs Grose that she was not at these times a child, but an old, old woman, and my description of her couldn't have been more strikingly confirmed than in the way in which, for all notice of this, she simply showed me, without an expressional concession or admission, a countenance of deeper and deeper, of indeed suddenly quite fixed reprobation. I was by this time – if I can put the whole

justified: proved right
an inarticulate message of gratitude: the writer is indicating that the Governess is grateful that Miss Jessel appears at this point because it will prove to Flora and Mrs Grose that she is not making the ghost up
The revelation then…I had expected: the Governess is shocked by Flora's calm reaction to the appearance of Miss Jessel
repress: stop
without…admission: without her expression changing
countenance: face
reprobation: accusation

COMMENTARY
The Governess thinks that, at last, Mrs Grose can see the ghosts. The Governess tries to get Flora to admit that Miss Jessel is there but Flora only looks straight at her with disapproval.

thing at all together – more appalled at what I may properly call her manner than at anything else, though it was quite simultaneously that I became aware of having Mrs Grose also, and very formidably, to reckon with. My elder companion, the next moment, at any rate, blotted out everything but her own flushed face and her loud shocked protest, a burst of high disapproval. 'What a dreadful turn, to be sure, Miss! Where on earth do you see anything?' ◄◄

I could only grasp her more quickly yet, for even while she spoke the hideous plain presence stood undimmed and undaunted. It had already lasted a minute, and it lasted while I continued, seizing my colleague, quite thrusting her at it and presenting her to it, to insist with my pointing hand. 'You don't see her exactly as *we* see? – you mean to say you don't now – *now*? She's as big as a blazing fire! Only look, dearest woman, *look*—!' She looked, just as I did, and gave me, with her deep groan of negation, repulsion, compassion – the mixture with her pity of her relief at her exemption – a sense, touching to me even then, that she would have backed me up if she had been able. I might well have needed that, for with this hard blow of the proof that her eyes were hopelessly sealed I felt my own situation horribly crumble. I felt – I *saw* – my livid predecessor press, from her position, on my defeat, and I took the measure, more than all, of what I should have from this instant to deal with in the astounding little attitude of Flora. Into this attitude Mrs Grose immediately and violently entered, breaking, even while there pierced through my sense of ruin a prodigious private triumph, into breathless reassurance.

'She isn't there, little lady, and nobody's there – and you never see nothing,

---

REWIND: …do you see anything?'

The Governess points out the ghost of Miss Jessel across the water: Mrs Grose *appears* to see it, but Flora refuses to look and instead gives the Governess a hard stare. The Governess is more shocked by this behaviour than by the sight of the ghost. It becomes clear that Mrs Grose *cannot* see the ghost and is wondering what the Governess is looking at.

◄◄

COMMENTARY

In fact, Mrs Grose is unable to see Miss Jessel and the Governess realises that this makes it difficult for her to believe her. Added to what she thinks is Flora's refusal to see the ghost, the Governess feels that Miss Jessel has defeated her.

exemption: inability to see the ghost
livid predecessor: Miss Jessel

my sweet! How can poor Miss Jessel – when poor Miss Jessel's dead and buried? *We* know, don't we, love?' – and she appealed, blundering in, to the child. 'It's all a mere mistake and a worry and a joke – and we'll go home as fast as we can!'

Our companion, on this, had responded with a strange quick primness of propriety, and they were again, with Mrs Grose on her feet, united, as it were, in shocked opposition to me. Flora continued to fix me with her small mask of disaffection, and even at that minute I prayed God to forgive me for seeming to see that, as she stood there holding tight to our friend's dress, her incomparable childish beauty had suddenly failed, had quite vanished. I've said it already – she was literally, she was hideously hard; she had turned common and almost ugly. 'I don't know what you mean. I see nobody. I see nothing. I never *have*. I think you're cruel. I don't like you!' Then, after this deliverance, which might have been that of a vulgarly pert little girl in the street, she hugged Mrs Grose more closely and buried in her skirts the dreadful little face. In this position she launched an almost furious wail. 'Take me away, take me away – oh take me away from *her*!'

'From *me*?' I panted.

'From you – from you!' she cried.

Even Mrs Grose looked across at me dismayed; while I had nothing to do but communicate again with the figure that, on the opposite bank, without a movement, as rigidly still as if catching, beyond the interval, our voices, was as vividly there for my disaster as it was not there for my service. The wretched child had spoken exactly as if she had got from some outside source each of her stabbing little words, and I could therefore, in the full despair of all I had to accept, but sadly shake my head at her. 'If I had ever doubted all my doubt would at present have gone. I've been living with the miserable truth, and now it has only too much closed round me. Of course I've lost you: I've interfered, and you've seen, under *her* dictation' – with which I faced, over the pool again, our infernal witness – 'the easy and perfect way to meet it. I've done my best, but I've lost you. Good-bye.' For Mrs Grose I had an imperative, an almost

COMMENTARY

Mrs Grose comforts Flora and tells her that Miss Jessel is not there and that it is all a 'mistake'. Flora tells the Governess that she thinks she is 'cruel' and wants Mrs Grose to take her away. The Governess tells Flora that Miss Jessel's influence over her is too strong and that she has lost the fight for her.

primness of propriety: innocence
small mask of disaffection: a face of disapproval
deliverance: speech
vulgarly pert: ordinary and over-confident
imperative: commanding

frantic 'Go, go!' before which, in infinite distress, but mutely possessed of the little girl and clearly convinced, in spite of her blindness that something awful had occurred and some collapse engulfed us, she retreated, by the way we had come, as fast as she could move.

FAST FORWARD: to page 134

Of what first happened when I was left alone I had no subsequent memory. I only knew that at the end of, I suppose, a quarter of an hour, an *odorous* dampness and roughness, chilling and piercing my trouble, had made me understand that I must have thrown myself, on my face, to the ground and given way to a wildness of grief. I must have lain there long and cried and wailed, for when I raised my head the day was almost done. I got up and looked a moment, through the twilight, at the grey pool and its blank haunted edge, and then I took, back to the house, my dreary and difficult course. When I reached the gate in the fence the boat, to my surprise, was gone, so that I had a fresh reflexion to make on Flora's extraordinary command of the situation. She passed that night, by the most tacit and, I should add, were not the word so grotesque a false note, the happiest of arrangements, with Mrs Grose. I saw neither of them on my return, but on the other hand I saw, as by an ambiguous compensation, a great deal of Miles. I saw – I can use no other phrase – so much of him that it fairly measured more than it had never measured. No evening I had passed at Bly was to have had the portentous quality of this one; in spite of which – and in spite also of the *deeper depths of consternation* that had opened beneath my feet – *there was literally, in the ebbing actual, an extraordinarily sweet sadness.* On reaching the house I had never so much as looked for the boy; I had simply gone straight to my room to change what I was wearing and to take in, at a glance, *such material testimony to Flora's rupture.* Her little belongings had all been removed.

COMMENTARY
Mrs Grose takes Flora back to the house leaving the Governess alone by the lake where she throws herself on the ground in despair. Finally, she returns to the house, where she finds that Flora's belongings have been removed from her room and taken to Mrs Grose's room.

odorous: smelly
deeper depths of consternation: greater worry
there was literally…sweet sadness: her horror at what had happened gave way to sadness
such material…rupture: the signs that she and Flora were no longer friends

When later, by the schoolroom fire, I was served with tea by the usual maid, I indulged, on the article of my other pupil, in no inquiry whatever. He had his freedom now – he might have it to the end! Well, he did have it; and it consisted – in part at least – of his coming in at about eight o'clock and sitting down with me in silence. On the removal of the tea-things I had blown out the candles and drawn my chair closer: I was conscious of a mortal coldness and felt as if I should never again be warm. So when he appeared I was sitting in the glow with my thoughts. He paused a moment by the door as if to look at me; then – as if to share them – came to the other side of the hearth and sank into a chair. We sat there in absolute stillness; yet he wanted, I felt, to
►► be with me.

REWIND: …be with me.
The Governess has finally left the lakeside and has returned to the house, where Flora's belongings have been removed from her room.
The Governess spends a long time by the fire in the schoolroom where she is joined by Miles, who comes in and sits in the chair opposite her in silence.

I indulged…no enquiry whatever: she
    does not ask where Miles is

COMMENTARY
The Governess takes her tea by the schoolroom fire and Miles comes in to join her. They sit together in complete silence.

21

Look out for...
- what Mrs Grose tells the Governess about what Flora has been saying.
- the moment when the Governess asks Mrs Grose to take Flora away. What does she hope will happen when she is alone with Miles?
- the Governess's worries about what Flora will say to the children's uncle.

Before a new day, in my room, had fully broken, my eyes opened to Mrs Grose, who had come to my bedside with worse news. Flora was so markedly feverish that an illness was perhaps at hand; she had passed a night of extreme unrest, a night agitated above all by fears that had for their subject not in the least her former but wholly her present governess. It was not against the possible re-entrance of Miss Jessel on the scene that she protested – it was conspicuously and passionately against mine. I was at once on my feet, and with an immense deal to ask; the more that my friend had discernibly now girded her loins to meet me afresh. This I felt as soon as I had put to her the question of her sense of the child's sincerity as against my own. 'She persists in denying to you that she saw, or has ever seen, anything?'

My visitor's trouble truly was great. 'Ah Miss, it isn't a matter on which I can push her! Yet it isn't either, I must say, as if I much needed to. It has made her, every inch of her, quite old.'

'Oh I see her perfectly from here. She resents, for all the world like some high little personage, the imputation on her truthfulness and, as it were, her

COMMENTARY
The next morning Mrs Grose tells the Governess that Flora is ill and that she does not want to see her. She goes on to say that the events at the lake have made Flora look very old.

conspicuously: obviously
had discernibly now girded her loins: had prepared herself
the imputation on her truthfulness: being thought of as a liar

respectability. "Miss Jessel indeed – *she*!" Ah she's "respectable", the chit! The impression she gave me there yesterday was, I assure you, the very strangest of all: it was quite beyond any of the others. I *did* put my foot in it! She'll never speak to me again.'

Hideous and obscure as it all was, it held Mrs Grose briefly silent; then she granted my point with a frankness which, I made sure, had more behind it. 'I think indeed, Miss, she never will. She do have a grand manner about it!'

'And that manner' – I summed it up – 'is practically what's the matter with her now.'

Oh that manner, I could see in my visitor's face, and not a little else besides! 'She asks me every three minutes if I think you're coming in.'

'I see – I see.' I too, on my side, had so much more than worked it out. 'Has she said to you since yesterday – except to repudiate her familiarity with anything so dreadful – a single other word about Miss Jessel?'

'Not one, Miss. And of course, you know,' my friend added, 'I took it from her by the lake that just then and there at least there *was* nobody.'

'Rather! And naturally you take it from her still.'

'I don't contradict her. What else can I do?'

'Nothing in the world! You've the cleverest little person to deal with. They've made them – their two friends, I mean – still cleverer even than nature did; for it was wondrous material to play on! Flora has now her grievance, and she'll work it to the end.'

'Yes, Miss; but to *what* end?'

'Why that of dealing with me to her uncle. She'll make me out to him the lowest creature—!'

I winced at the fair show of the scene in Mrs Grose's face; she looked for a minute as if she sharply saw them together. 'And him who thinks so well of you!'

'He had an odd way – it comes over me now,' I laughed, '—of proving it! But that doesn't matter. What Flora wants of course is to get rid of me.'

My companion bravely concurred. 'Never again to so much as look at you.'

'So that what you've come to me now for,' I asked, 'is to speed me on my

---

the chit: a disrespectful girl

I did put my foot in it: by mentioning Miss Jessel

And that manner…with her now: her illness is only a way of keeping the Governess away

repudiate her familiarity: deny her knowledge

They've made them…than nature did: Quint and Miss Jessel have made the children able to trick Mrs Grose and the Governess

COMMENTARY
Mrs Grose tells the Governess that Flora continues to deny that she saw anything by the lake and that she does not want to see the Governess again. The Governess thinks that Flora, by appearing to be upset, is plotting to get rid of her. If the uncle has to come to Bly the Governess can be accused of making Flora ill by frightening her with stories about ghosts.

way?' Before she had time to reply, however, I had her in check. 'I've a better idea – the result of my reflexions. My going *would* seem the right thing, and on Sunday I was terribly near it. Yet that won't do. It's *you* who must go. You must take Flora.'

My visitor, at this, did speculate. 'But where in the world—?'

'Away from here. Away from *them*. Away, even most of all, now, from me. Straight to her uncle.'

'Only to tell on you—?'

'No, not "only"! To leave me, in addition, with my remedy.'

She was still vague. 'And what *is* your remedy?'

'Your loyalty, to begin with. And then Miles's.'

She looked at me hard. 'Do you think he—?'

'Won't, if he has the chance, turn on me? Yes, I venture still to think it. At all events I want to try. Get off with his sister as soon as possible and leave me with him alone.' I was amazed, myself, at the spirit I had still in reserve, and therefore perhaps a trifle the more disconcerted at the way in which, in spite of this fine example of it, she hesitated. 'There's one thing, of course,' I went on: 'they mustn't, before she goes, see each other for three seconds.' Then it came over me that, in spite of Flora's presumable sequestration from the instant to her return from the pool, it might already be too late. 'Do you mean,' I anxiously asked, 'that they *have* met?'

At this she quite flushed. 'Ah, Miss, I'm not such a fool as that! If I've been obliged to leave her three or four times, it has been each time with one of the maids, and at present, though she's alone, she's locked in safe. And yet – and yet!' There were too many things.

'And yet what?'

'Well, are you so sure of the little gentleman?'

'I'm not sure of anything but *you*. But I have since last evening, a new hope. I think he wants to give me an opening. I do believe that – poor little exquisite wretch! – he wants to speak. Last evening, in the firelight and the silence, he sat with me for two hours as if it were just coming.'

COMMENTARY

The Governess proposes that Mrs Grose takes Flora away to the uncle's house in London. She is prepared to risk being talked about by Flora because she wants to be alone with Miles, whom she thinks is ready to tell her *everything*.

at the spirit I had still in reserve: the courage she still had

a trifle the more disconcerted: a little more surprised

sequestration: kept secretly and away from the rest of the household

Mrs Grose looked hard through the window at the grey gathering day. 'And did it come?'

'No, though I waited and waited I confess it didn't, and it was without a breach of the silence, or so much as a faint allusion to his sister's condition and absence, that we at last kissed for goodnight. All the same,' I continued, 'I can't, if her uncle sees her, consent to his seeing her brother without my having given the boy – and most of all because things have go so bad – a little more time.'

My friend appeared on this ground more reluctant than I could quite understand. 'What do you mean by more time?'

'Well, a day or two – really to bring it out. He'll then be on *my* side – of which you see the importance. If nothing comes I shall only fail, and you at the worst have helped me by doing on your arrival in town whatever you may have found possible' So I put it before her, but she continued for a little so lost in other reasons that I came again to her aid. 'Unless indeed,' I wound up, 'you really want *not* to go.'

I could see it, in her face, at last clear itself: she put out her hand to me as a pledge. 'I'll go – I'll go. I'll go this morning.'

I wanted to be very just. 'If you *should* wish still to wait I'd engage she shouldn't see me.'

'No, no: it's the place itself. She must leave it.' She held me a moment with heavy eyes, then brought out the rest. 'Your idea's the right one. I myself, Miss—'

'Well?'

'I can't stay.'

The look she gave me with it made me jump at possibilities. 'You mean that, since yesterday, you *have* seen—?'

She shook her head with dignity. 'I've *heard*—!'

'Heard?'

'From that child – horrors! There!' she sighed with tragic relief. 'On my honour, Miss, she says things—!' But at this evocation she broke down; she

breach: break
faint allusion: mentioning the
    subject vaguely

COMMENTARY
By staying at Bly with Miles the Governess hopes to get him on her side so that they can face the ghosts together. Mrs Grose agrees to take Flora away and adds that, in any case, she cannot stay.

dropped with a sudden cry upon my sofa and, as I had seen her do before, gave way to all the anguish of it.

It was quite in another manner that I for my part let myself go. 'Oh thank God!'

She sprang up again at this, drying her eyes with a groan. '"Thank God"?'

'It so justifies me!'

'It does that, Miss!'

I couldn't have desired more emphasis, but I just waited. 'She's so horrible?'

I saw my colleague scarce knew how to put it. 'Really shocking.'

'And about me?'

'About you, Miss – since you must have it. It's beyond everything, for a young lady; and I can't think wherever she must have picked up—'

'The appalling language she applies to me? I can, then!' I broke in with a laugh that was doubtless significant enough.

It only in truth left my friend still more grave. 'Well, perhaps I ought to also – since I've heard some of it before! Yet I can't bear it,' the poor woman went on while with the same movement she glanced, on my dressing-table, at the face of my watch. 'But I must go back.'

I kept her, however. 'Ah if you can't bear it—!'

'How can I stop with her, you mean? Why just *for* that: to get her away. Far from this,' she pursued, 'far from *them*—'

'She may be different? She may be free?' I seized her almost with joy. 'Then in spite of yesterday you *believe*—'

'In such doings?' Her simple description of them required, in the light of her expression, to be carried no farther, and she gave me the whole thing as she had never done. 'I believe.'

FAST FORWARD: to page 141

grave: serious

COMMENTARY

Mrs Grose explains to the Governess that she has heard Flora saying horrifying things about the Governess and using very bad language. The Governess is relieved because this proves that the children are under the influence of Quint and Miss Jessel, despite their denials. She is also delighted that, at last, Mrs Grose accepts her version of the events at Bly.

Yes, it was a joy, and we were still shoulder to shoulder: if I might continue sure of that I should care but little what else happened. My support in the presence of disaster would be the same as it had been in my early need of confidence, and if my friend would answer for my honesty I would answer for all the rest. On the point of taking leave of her, none the less, I was to some extent embarrassed. 'There's one thing of course – it occurs to me – to remember. My letter giving the alarm will have reached town before you.'

I now felt still more how she had been beating about the bush and how weary at last it had made her. 'Your letter won't have got there. Your letter never went.'

'What, then, became of it?'

'Goodness knows! Master Miles—'

'Do you mean *he* took it?' I gasped.

She hung fire, but she overcame her reluctance. 'I mean that I saw yesterday, when I came back with Miss Flora, that it wasn't where you had put it. Later in the evening I had the chance to question Luke, and he declared that he had neither noticed nor touched it.' We could only exchange, on this, one of our deeper mutual soundings, and it was Mrs Grose who first brought up the plumb with an almost elate 'You see!'

'Yes, I see that if Miles took it instead he probably will have read it and destroyed it.'

'And don't you see anything else?'

I faced her a moment with a sad smile. 'It strikes me that by this time your eyes are open even wider than mine.'

They proved to be so indeed, but she could still almost blush to show it. 'I make out now what he must have done at school.' And she gave, in her simple sharpness, an almost droll disillusioned nod. 'He stole!'

I turned it over – I tried to be more judicial. 'Well – perhaps.'

She looked as if she found me unexpectedly calm. 'He stole *letters*!'

She couldn't know my reasons for a calmness after all pretty shallow; so I showed them off as I might. 'I hope, then, it was to more purpose than in this

and if my friend would answer for my honesty: if Mrs Grose would tell the uncle that she was telling the truth about the ghosts and their influence over the children

She hung fire: hesitated

plumb: a lead weight used for measuring – the word is used here to suggest bringing the truth to the surface

elate: joyful

droll disillusioned nod: an amused but disappointed nod

She couldn't know…pretty shallow: she is calm at the news about the letter only because she knows that there is nothing important in it

COMMENTARY
Mrs Grose tells the Governess that her letter to the uncle was never sent and that she thinks Miles stole it. She has concluded that stealing letters must have been the reason why he was expelled from school.

case! The note, at all events, that I put on the table yesterday,' I pursued, 'will have given him so scant an advantage – for it contained only the bare demand for an interview – that he's already much ashamed of having gone so far for so little, and that what he had on his mind last evening was precisely the need of confession.' I seemed to myself for the instant to have mastered it, to see it all. 'Leave us, leave us' – I was already, at the door, hurrying her off. 'I'll get it out of him. He'll meet me. He'll confess. If he confesses he's saved. And if he's saved—'

'Then *you* are?' The dear woman kissed me on this, and I took her farewell. 'I'll save you without him!' she cried as she went.   ◀◀

REWIND: …as she went.

Mrs Grose has told the Governess that her letter to the children's uncle was not sent and that Miles took it from the hall table. Mrs Grose has come to the conclusion that Miles was expelled for stealing letters. The Governess hopes that, when Mrs Grose and Flora have left Bly, Miles will confess everything and so be saved from the evil influence of the ghosts.

COMMENTARY

The Governess thinks that Miles may have sat with her the previous evening to confess that he had stolen the letter. She is keen to be alone with him so that she can get at the truth about what has been happening at Bly.

scant: little

I'll save you without him: Mrs Grose is offering to tell the uncle that she has discovered what has been going on at Bly – even though it is hard to believe. In this way the Governess's reputation with the uncle will be 'saved'

22

Look out for...
● **the Governess's feelings on being left alone with Miles at Bly.**

FAST FORWARD: to page 144

Yet it was when she had got off – and I missed her on the spot – that the great pinch really came. If I had counted on what it would give me to find myself alone with Miles I quickly recognised that it would give me at least a measure. No hour of my stay in fact was so assailed with apprehensions as that of my coming down to learn that the carriage contained Mrs Grose and my younger pupil had already rolled out of the gates. Now I *was*, I said to myself, face to face with the elements, and for much of the rest of the day, while I fought my weakness, I could consider that I had been supremely rash. It was a tighter place still than I had yet turned round in; all the more that, for the first time, I could see in the aspect of others a confused reflexion of the crisis. What had happened naturally caused them all to stare; there was too little of the explained, throw out whatever we might, in the suddenness of my colleague's

the great pinch: the reality of the situation
recognised that...a measure: she realises that she has never felt so nervous
face to face with the elements: facing the challenge of Quint and Miss Jessel for possession of Miles and Flora
been supremely rash: made a big mistake

COMMENTARY
Mrs Grose and Flora leave Bly and the Governess is nervous about facing the task ahead alone. She notices that the servants are confused about the departure of the housekeeper and the little girl.

act. The maids and the men looked blank; the effect of which on my nerves was an aggravation until I saw the necessity of making it a positive aid. It was in short by just clutching the helm that I avoided total wreck; and I daresay that, to bear up at all, I became that morning very grand and very dry. I welcomed the consciousness that I was charged with much to do, and I caused it to be known as well that, left thus to myself, I was quite remarkably firm. I wandered with that manner, for the next hour or two, all over the place and looked, I have no doubt, as if I were ready for any onset. So, for the benefit of whom it might concern, I paraded with a sick heart.

The person it appeared least to concern proved to be, till dinner, little Miles himself. My perambulations had given me meanwhile no glimpse of him, but they had tended to make more public the change taking place in our relation as a consequence of his having at the piano, the day before, kept me, in Flora's interest, so beguiled and befooled. The stamp of publicity had of course been fully given by her confinement and departure, and the change itself was now ushered in by our non-observance of the regular custom of the schoolroom. He

COMMENTARY

The Governess puts on a brave face and behaves as if there is no problem. However, Flora's departure and Miles's new freedom from his lessons makes it obvious that things have changed.

by just clutching…total wreck: by taking control of the situation the Governess was able to put her fears behind her

onset: problem

perambulations: walks

but they had tended…beguiled and befooled: Miles has fooled the Governess by playing the piano so that Flora could escape, and as a result the relationship between Miles and the Governess has changed – the Governess's attempts to find Miles makes this change obvious to everyone in the house

ushered in…of the schoolroom: signalled by not doing lessons in the schoolroom

had already disappeared when, on my way down, I pushed open his door, and I learned below that he had breakfasted – in the presence of a couple of the maids – with Mrs Grose and his sister. He had then gone out, as he said, for a stroll; than which nothing, I reflected, could better have expressed his frank view of the abrupt transformation of my office. What he would now permit this office to consist of was yet to be settled: there was at the least a queer relief – I mean for myself in especial – in the renouncement of one pretension. If so much had sprung to the surface I scarce put it too strongly in saying that what had perhaps sprung highest was the absurdity of our prolonging the fiction that I had anything more to teach him. It sufficiently stuck out that, by tacit little tricks in which even more than myself he carried out the care for my dignity. I had had to appeal to him to let me off straining to meet him on the ground of his true capacity. He had at any rate his freedom now, I was never to touch it again: as I had amply shown, moreover, when, on his joining me in the schoolroom the previous night, I uttered, in reference to the interval just concluded, neither challenge nor hint. I had too much, from this moment, my other ideas. Yet when he at last arrived the difficulty of applying them, the accumulations of my problem, were brought straight home to me by the beautiful little presence on which what had occurred had as yet, for the eye, ▶▶ dropped neither stain nor shadow.

To mark, for the house, the high state I cultivated I decreed that my meals with the boy should be served, as we called it, downstairs; so that I had been

---

REWIND: …stain nor shadow.
After Mrs Grose and Flora have gone, the Governess feels nervous about being left to fight the influence of the ghosts on her own. She is busy and bright around the house so that the servants do not think anything unusual has happened. Miles has had breakfast with Mrs Grose and his sister before they leave and, instead of going to lessons, has then gone out for a walk. The Governess does not mind this as she realises that he has grown out of her teaching.

---

than which nothing…of my office: by not asking the Governess's permission to go for a walk, Miles is showing his new independence
renouncement: giving up
absurdity: silliness
prolonging: carrying on
It sufficiently stuck out…his true capacity: despite Miles's attempts at saving her dignity, the Governess had to admit that her knowledge and understanding was not as good as his

COMMENTARY
Miles has gone out for a walk and the Governess realises that he will no longer attend lessons. To mark the change in their relationship the Governess decides that they will have their meals together in the dining hall, like two adults.

awaiting him in the ponderous pomp of the room outside the window of which I had had from Mrs Grose, that first scared Sunday, my flash of something it would scarce have done to call light. Here at present I felt afresh – for I had felt it again and again – how my equilibrium depended on the success of rigid will, the will to shut my eyes as tight as possible to the truth that what I had to deal with was, revoltingly, against nature. I could only get on at all by taking 'nature' into my confidence and my account, by treating my monstrous ordeal as a push in a direction unusual, of course, and unpleasant, but demanding after all, for a fair front, only another turn of the screw of ordinary human virtue. No attempt, none the less, could well require more tact than just this attempt to supply, one's self, *all* the nature. How could I put even a little of that article into a suppression of reference to what had occurred? How, on the other hand, could I make a reference without a new plunge into the hideous obscure? Well, a sort of answer, after a time, had come to me, and it was so far confirmed as that I was met, incontestably, by the quickened vision of what was rare in my little companion. It was indeed as if he had found even now – as he had so often found at lessons – still some other delicate way to ease me off. Wasn't there light in the fact which, as we shared our solitude, broke out with a specious glitter it had never yet quite worn? – the fact that (opportunity aiding, precious opportunity which had now come) it would be preposterous, with a child so endowed, to forgo the help one might wrest from absolute intelligence? What had his intelligence been given him for but to save him? Mightn't one, to reach his mind, risk the stretch of a stiff arm across his character? It was as if, when we were face to face in the dining-room, he had literally shown me the way. The roast mutton was on the table and I had dispensed with attendance. Miles, before he sat down, stood a moment with his hands in his pockets and looked at the joint, on which he seemed on the point of passing some humorous judgement. But what he presently produced was: 'I say, my dear, is she really very awfully ill?'

'Little Flora? Not so bad but that she'll presently be better. London will set her up. Bly had ceased to agree with her. Come here and take your mutton.'

COMMENTARY

Miles and the Governess have met in the dining hall for a meal. The Governess is determined to get Miles to confess all and hopes that his superior intelligence will help her to get him to do this. Miles opens the conversation by asking about Flora.

ponderous pomp: formality

how my equilibrium...rigid will: keeping her nerve depended on great self control

against nature: unnatural

by treating my monstrous...ordinary human virtue: the Governess's sense of what is right and good is the only way that she is going to be able to defeat the evil ghosts

How could I put...hideous obscure: if she does mention Quint or Miss Jessel she is afraid that Miles will react like Flora *but* if she does not talk about Quint's ghost directly then she will never be able to rescue Miles from him

specious glitter: falsely appealing

He alertly obeyed me, carried the plate carefully to his seat and, when he was established, went on: 'Did Bly disagree with her so terribly all at once?'

'No so suddenly as you might think. One had seen it coming on.'

'Then why didn't you get her off before?'

'Before what?'

'Before she became too ill to travel.'

I found myself prompt. 'She's *not* too ill to travel; she only might have become so if she had stayed. This was just the moment to seize. The journey will dissipate the influence' – oh I was grand! – 'and carry it off.'

'I see, I see' – Miles, for that matter, was grand too. He settled to his repast with the charming little 'table manner' that, from the day of his arrival, had relieved me of all grossness of admonition. Whatever he had been expelled from school for, it wasn't for ugly feeding. He was irreproachable, as always, to-day; but was unmistakably more conscious. He was discernibly trying to take for granted more things than he found, without assistance, quite easy; and he dropped into peaceful silence while he felt his situation. Our meal was of the briefest – mine a vain pretence, and I had the things immediately removed. While this was done Miles stood again with his hands in his little pockets and his back to me – stood and looked out of the wide window through which, that other day, I had seen what pulled me up. We continued silent while the maid was with us – as silent, it whimsically occurred to me, as some young couple who, on their wedding-journey, at the inn, feel shy in the presence of the waiter. He turned round only when the waiter had left us. 'Well – so we're alone!'

---

dissipate: weaken

relieved me of all grossness of admonition: she had never had to tell him off about his table manners

He was discernibly…quite easy: Miles was now showing the Governess that he was more independent

COMMENTARY

The Governess explains that by leaving Bly, Flora will get better. They eat their meal in silence, the servants clear it away and they are left alone.

23

Look out for...
● the way in which Miles seems ready to confess everything but the Governess is nervous about bringing up the subject of the ghosts. Notice how they approach the subject and the importance of the Governess's descriptions of Miles and her feelings at this point in the story.

'Oh more or less,' I imagine my smile was pale. 'Not absolutely. We shouldn't like that!' I went on.

'No – I suppose we shouldn't. Of course we've the others.'

'We've the others – we've indeed the others,' I concurred.

'Yet even though we have them' he returned, still with his hands in his pockets and planted there in front of me, 'they don't much count, do they?'

Made the best of it, but I felt wan. 'It depends on what you call "much"!'

'Yes' – with all accommodation – 'everything depends!' On this, however, he faced to the window again and presently reached it with his vague restless cogitating step. He remained there a while with his forehead against the glass, in contemplation of the stupid shrubs I knew and the dull things of November. I had always my hypocrisy of 'work', behind which I now gained the sofa. Steadying myself with it there as I had repeatedly done at those moments of torment that I have described as the moments of my knowing the children to be given to something from which I was barred, I sufficiently obeyed my habit of being prepared for the worst. But an extraordinary impression dropped on

COMMENTARY
The Governess and Miles talk about not being completely alone but it is unclear whether the 'others' are the servants in the house or Quint and Miss Jessel.

wan: pale

cogitating: thoughtful

the moments of my knowing…from which I was barred: the children's communication with the ghosts from which the Governess is left out

me as I extracted a meaning from the boy's embarrassed back – none other than the impression that I was not barred now. This inference grew in a few minutes to sharp intensity and seemed bound up with the direct perception that it was positively *he* who was. The frames and squares of the great window were a kind of image, for him, of a kind of failure. I felt that I saw him, in any case, shut in or shut out. He was admirable but not comfortable: I took it in with a throb of hope. Wasn't he looking through the haunted pane for something he couldn't see? – and wasn't it the first time in the whole business that he had known such a lapse? The first, the very first: I found it a splendid portent. It made him anxious, though he watched himself; he had been anxious all day and, even while in his usual sweet little manner he sat at table, had needed all his small strange genius to give it a gloss. When he at last turned round to meet me it was almost as if this genius had succumbed. 'Well, I think I'm glad Bly agrees with *me*!'

'You'd certainly seem to have seen, these twenty-four hours, a good deal more of than for some time before. I hope' I went on bravely, 'that you've been enjoying yourself.'

'Oh yes, I've been ever so far; all round about – miles and miles away. I've never been so free.'

He had really a manner of his own, and I could only try to keep up with him. 'Well, do you like it?'

He stood there smiling; then at last he put into two words – 'Do *you*?' – more discrimination than I had ever heard two words contain. Before I had time to deal with that, however, he continued as if with the sense that this was an impertinence to be softened. 'Nothing could be more charming than the way you take it, for of course if we're alone together now it's you that are alone most. But I hope,' he threw in, 'you don't particularly mind!'

'Having to do with you?' I asked. 'My dear child, how can I help minding? Though I've renounced all claim to your company – you're so beyond me – I at least greatly enjoy it. What else should I stay on for?'

He looked at me more directly, and the expression of his face, graver now,

inference: understanding
direct perception: understanding
portent: sign
had needed…it a gloss: all his skill
    to hide his feelings
this genius had succumbed: his
    skill had failed
discrimination: understanding
impertinence: cheekinesss

COMMENTARY
Miles is staring out of the same window through which the Governess saw Quint. She has the impression that he is looking for Quint. He seems unable to 'see' him and this encourages the Governess to think that Miles has lost touch with what she thinks is his evil influence. Miles asks whether the Governess minds that he is no longer under her direct control.

struck me as the most beautiful I had ever found in it. 'You stay on just for *that*?'

'Certainly. I stay on as your friend and from the tremendous interest I take in you till something can be done for you that may be more worth your while. That needn't surprise you.' My voice trembled so that I felt it impossible to suppress the shake. 'Don't you remember how I told you, when I came and sat on your bed the night of the storm, that there was nothing in the world I wouldn't do for you?'

'Yes, yes!' He, on his side, more and more visibly nervous, had a tone to master; but he was so much more successful than I that, laughing out through his gravity, he could pretend we were pleasantly jesting. 'Only that, I think, was to get me to do something for *you*!'

'It was partly to get you to do something,' I conceded. 'But, you know, you didn't do it.'

'Oh yes,' he said with the brightest superficial eagerness, 'you wanted me to tell you something.'

'That's it. Out, straight out. What you have on your mind, you know.'

'Ah, then, is *that* what you've stayed over for?'

He spoke with a gaiety through which I could still catch the finest little quiver of resentful passion; but I can't begin to express the effect upon me of an implication of surrender even so faint. It was as if what I had yearned for had come at last only to astonish me. 'Well, yes – I may as well make a clean breast of it. It was precisely for that.'

He waited so long that I supposed it for the purpose of repudiating the assumption on which my action had been founded; but what he finally said was: 'Do you mean now – here?'

'There couldn't be a better place or time.' He looked round him uneasily, and I had the rare – oh the queer! impression of the very first symptom I had seen in him of the approach of immediate fear. It was as if he were suddenly afraid of me – which struck me indeed as perhaps the best thing to make him. Yet in the very pang of the effort I felt it vain to try sternness, and I heard myself the

COMMENTARY

The Governess tells Miles that she has stayed at Bly because she wants him to tell her everything: Whether that means the reason he was expelled or his relationship with Quint she does not make clear. Miles appears to be frightened by being asked to confess so directly.

gravity: seriousness
jesting: joking
superficial: easy
gaiety: happiness
quiver of resentful passion: hint of resentment
repudiating the assumption…had been founded: denying that he had anything to tell her

next instant so gentle as to be almost grotesque. 'You want so to go out again?'

'Awfully!' He smiled at me heroically, and the touching little bravery of it was enhanced by his actually flushing with pain. He had picked up his hat, which he had brought in, and stood twirling it in a way that gave me, even as I was just nearly reaching port, a perverse horror of what I was doing. To do it in *any* way was an act of violence, for what did it consist of but the obtrusion of the idea of grossness and guilt on a small helpless creature who had been for me a revelation of the possibilities of beautiful intercourse? Wasn't it base to create for a being so exquisite a mere alien awkwardness? I suppose I now read into our situation a clearness it couldn't have had at the time, for I seem to see our poor eyes already lighted with some spark of a prevision of the anguish that was to come. So we circled about with terrors and scruples, fighters but not daring to close. But it was for each other we feared! That kept us a little longer suspended and unbruised. 'I'll tell you everything,' Miles said – 'I mean I'll tell you anything you like. You'll stay on with me, and we shall both be all right, and I *will* tell you – I *will*. But not now.'

'Why not now?'

My insistence turned him from me and kept him once more at his window in a silence during which, between us, you might have heard a pin drop. Then he was before me again with the air of a person for whom, outside, someone who had frankly to be reckoned with was waiting. 'I have to see Luke.'

I had not yet reduced him to quite so vulgar a lie, and I felt proportionately ashamed. But, horrible as it was, his lies made up my truth. I achieved thoughtfully a few loops of my knitting. 'Well then, go to Luke, and I'll wait for what you promise. Only in return for that satisfy, before you leave me, one very much smaller request.'

He looked as if he felt he had succeeded enough to be able still a little to bargain. 'Very much smaller—?'

'Yes, a mere fraction of the whole. Tell me' – oh my work preoccupied me, and I was off-hand! – 'if yesterday afternoon, from the table in the hall, you took, you know, my letter.'

---

enhanced: added to
reaching port: getting an answer
obtrusion: introduction
revelation…intercourse: the Governess is thinking
   of when she arrived at Bly and how beautiful
   and innocent the children seemed
base: horrible
alien awkwardness: unfamiliar difficulty
prevision: a view of the future
scruples: doubts

COMMENTARY

The Governess has a sudden doubt about forcing this beautiful little boy to talk about evil and ugly things. He asks to go and see Luke and the Governess says he may if he tells her whether or not he took her letter.

24

My grasp of how he received this suffered for a minute from something that I can describe only as a fierce split of my attention – a stroke that at first, as I sprang straight up, reduced me to the mere blind movement of getting hold of him, drawing him close and, while I just fell for support against the nearest piece of furniture, instinctively keeping him with his back to the window. The appearance was full upon us that I had already had to deal with here: Peter Quint had come into view like a sentinel before a prison. The next thing I saw was that, from outside, he had reached the window, and then I knew that, close to the glass and glaring in through it, he offered once more to the room his white face of damnation. It represents but grossly what took place within me at the sight to say that on the second my decision was made; yet I believe that no woman so overwhelmed ever in so short a time recovered her command of the *act*. It came to me in the very horror of the immediate presence that the act would be, seeing and facing what I saw and faced, to keep the boy himself unaware. The inspiration – I can call it by no other name – was that I felt how voluntarily, how transcendently, I *might*. It was like

COMMENTARY
Quint now appears at the window and the Governess grabs Miles and turns him away.

sentinel: guard
the immediate presence: Quint
transcendently: completely

fighting with a demon for a human soul, and when I had fairly so appraised it I saw how the human soul – held out, in the tremor of my hands, at arms' length – had a perfect dew of sweat on a lovely childish forehead. The face that was close to mine was as white as the face against the glass, and out of it presently came a sound, not low nor weak, but as if from much farther away, that I drank like a waft of fragrance.

'Yes – I took it.'

At this, with a moan of joy, I enfolded, I drew him close; and while I held him to my breast, where I could feel in the sudden fever of his little body the tremendous pulse of his little heart, I kept my eyes on the thing at the window and saw it move and shift its posture. I have likened it to a sentinel, but its slow wheel, for a moment, was rather the prowl of a baffled beast. My present quickened courage, however, was such that, not too much to let it through, I had to shade, as it were, my flame. Meanwhile the glare of the face was again at the window, the scoundrel fixed as if to watch and wait. It was the very confidence that I might now defy him, as well as the positive certitude, by this time, of the child's unconsciousness, that made me go on. 'What did you take it for?'

'To see what you said about me.'

'You opened the letter?'

'I opened it.'

My eyes were now, as I held him off a little again, on Miles's own face, in which the collapse of mockery showed me how complete was the ravage of uneasiness. What was prodigious was that at last, by my success, his sense was sealed and his communication stopped: he knew that he was in presence, but knew not of what, and knew still less that I also was and that I did know. And what did this strain of trouble matter when my eyes went back to the window only to see that the air was clear again and – by my personal triumph – the influence quenched? There was nothing there. I felt that the cause was mine and that I should surely get *all*. 'And you found nothing!' – I let my elation out.

appraised: seen
I drank like a waft of fragrance: Miles's expression is very sweet to the Governess
posture: position
My present quickened courage…my flame: the Governess does not want to show her fierce courage to Miles in case it frightens him
It was the very…child's unconsciousness: the Governess's ability to challenge Quint is strengthened by Miles's inability to 'see' him
in which the collapse…ravage of uneasiness: behind Miles's pretence at innocence was a very disturbed mind

COMMENTARY
Miles confesses that he took the letter but the Governess is also aware that he is no longer able to 'see' the ghost of Quint who is moving up and down uneasily on the other side of the window. He disappears when Miles makes his confession and the Governess feels that she has won the battle for control of Miles.

He gave the most mournful thoughtful little headshake. 'Nothing'.

'Nothing, nothing!' I almost shouted in my joy.

'Nothing, nothing,' he sadly repeated.

I kissed his forehead; it was drenched. 'So what have you done with it?'

'I've burnt it.'

'Burnt it?' It was now or never. 'Is that what you did at school?'

Oh what this brought up! 'At school?'

'Did you take letters? – or other things?'

'Other things?' He appeared now to be thinking of something far off and that reached him only through the pressure of his anxiety. Yet it did reach him. 'Did I *steal*?'

I felt myself redden to the roots of my hair as well as wonder if it were more strange to put to a gentleman such a question or to see him take it with allowances that gave the very distance of his fall in the world. 'Was it for that you mightn't go back?'

The only thing he felt was rather a dreary little surprise. 'Did you know I mightn't go back?'

'I know everything.'

He gave me at this the longest and strangest look. 'Everything?'

'Everything. Therefore *did* you—?' But I couldn't say it again.

Miles could, very simply. 'No. I didn't steal.'

My face must have shown him I believed him utterly; yet my hands – but it was for pure tenderness – shook him as if to ask him why, if it was all for nothing, he had condemned me to months of torment. 'What, then, did you do?'

He looked in vague pain all round the top of the room and drew his breath, two or three times over, as if with difficulty. He might have been standing at the bottom of the sea and raising his eyes to some faint green twilight. 'Well – I said things.'

'Only that?'

'They thought it was enough!'

'To turn you out for?'

to put to a…his fall in the world: to ask the question or see his expression which showed how bad he had been

COMMENTARY

Miles tells the Governess that he found nothing important in the letter and burnt it. The Governess asks if he was expelled from school for stealing. Miles denies this.

Never, truly, had a person 'turned out' shown so little to explain it as this little person! He appeared to weigh my question, but in a manner quite detached and almost helpless. 'Well, I suppose I oughtn't.'

'But to whom did you say them?'

He evidently tried to remember, but it dropped – he had lost it. 'I don't know!'

He almost smiled at me in the desolation of his surrender, which was indeed practically, by this time, so complete that I ought to have left it there. But I was infatuated – I was blind with victory, though even then the very effect that was to have brought him so much nearer was already that of added separation. 'Was it to everyone?' I asked.

'No; it was only to—' But he gave a sick little headshake. 'I don't remember their names.'

'Were they, then, so many?'

'No – only a few. Those I liked.'

Those he liked? I seemed to float, not into clearness, but into a darker obscure, and within a minute there had come to me out of my very pity the appalling alarm of his being perhaps innocent. It was for the instant confounding and bottomless, for if he *were* innocent what then on earth was I? Paralysed, while it lasted, by the mere brush of the question, I let him go a little, so that, with a deep-drawn sigh, he turned away from me again; which, as he faced toward the clear window, I suffered, feeling that I had nothing now there to keep him from. 'And did they repeat what you said?' I went on after a moment.

He was soon at some distance from me, still breathing hard and again with the air, though now without anger for it, of being confined against his will. Once more, as he had done before, he looked up at the dim day as if, of what had hitherto sustained him, nothing was left but an unspeakable anxiety. 'Oh yes,' he nevertheless replied – 'they must have repeated them. To those *they* liked,' he added.

There was somehow less of it than I had expected; but I turned it over. 'And these things came round—?'

desolation: sadness
obscure: uncertainty
hitherto sustained him: up to now
   kept him going

COMMENTARY

However, Miles does say that he had been expelled for 'saying things' to his friends but is no more precise. The Governess has a sudden doubt when she hears this – perhaps he is innocent? Trying to remember what actually happened at school makes Miles anxious and sad.

'To the masters? Oh yes!' he answered very simply. 'But I didn't know they'd tell.'

'The masters? They didn't – they've never told. That's why I ask you.'

He turned to me again his little beautiful fevered face. 'Yes, it was too bad.'

'Too bad?'

'What I suppose I sometimes said. To write home.'

I can't name the exquisite pathos of the contradiction given to such a speech by such a speaker; I only know that the next instant I heard myself throw off with homely force: 'Stuff and nonsense!' But the next after that I must have sounded stern enough. 'What *were* these things?'

My sternness was all for his judge, his executioner; yet it made him avert himself again, and that moment made *me*, with a single bound and an irrepressible cry, spring straight upon him. For there again, against the glass, as if to blight his confession and stay his answer, was the hideous author of our woe – the white face of damnation. I felt a sick swim at the drop of my victory and all the return of my battle, so that the wildness of my veritable leap only served as a great betrayal. I saw him, from the midst of my act, meet it with a divination, and on the perception that even now he only guessed, and that the window was still to his own eyes free, I let the impulse flame up to convert the climax of his dismay into the very proof of his liberation. 'No more, no more, no more!' I shrieked to my visitant as I tried to press him against me.

'Is she *here*?' Miles panted as he caught with his sealed eyes the direction of my words. Then as his strange 'she' staggered me and, with a gasp, I echoed it, 'Miss Jessel, Miss Jessel!' he with sudden fury gave me back.

I seized, stupefied, his supposition – some sequel to what we had done to Flora, but this made me only want to show him that it was better still than that. 'It's not Miss Jessel! But it's at the window – straight before us. It's *there* – the coward horror, there for the last time!'

At this, after a second in which his head made the movement of a baffled dog's on a scent and then gave a frantic little shake for air and light, he was at me in a white rage, bewildered, glaring vainly over the place and missing

COMMENTARY

The Governess asks him what 'things' he said at school. Miles does not answer and turns away to the window. The next moment she leaps at him as the figure of Quint appears again. Miles surprises her by asking if the face at the window is Miss Jessel's.

his judge, his executioner: Quint
served as a great betrayal: her action tells Miles that Quint has reappeared
divination: understanding
I let the impulse...of his liberation: Miles's confusion at her actions proved that he could no longer 'see' Quint and so was free of his influence

wholly, though it now, to my sense, filled the room like the taste of poison, the wide overwhelming presence. 'It's *he*?'

I was so determined to have all my proof that I flashed into ice to challenge him. 'Whom do you mean by "he"?'

'Peter Quint – you devil!' His face gave again, round the room, its convulsed supplication. '*Where*?'

They are in my ears still, his supreme surrender of the name and his tribute to my devotion. 'What does he matter now, my own? – what will he *ever* matter? *I* have you,' I launched at the beast, 'but he has lost you for ever!' Then for the demonstration of my work, 'There, *there*!' I said to Miles.

But he had already jerked straight round, stared, glared again, and seen but the quiet day. With the stroke of the loss I was so proud of he uttered the cry of a creature hurled over an abyss, and the grasp with which I recovered him might have been that of catching him in his fall. I caught him, yes, I held him – it may be imagined with what a passion; but at the end of a minute I began to feel what it truly was that I held. We were alone with the quiet day, and his little heart, dispossessed, had stopped.

convulsed supplication:
  tortured pleading

Study guide

How to use this Study guide

This Study guide is divided into six sections. Each of the first five looks at several chapters of the story. The final section looks at the story as a whole. In sections 1 to 5, there are three types of material:

Tracking: These questions take you through the chapters and give you ideas to think about.

Character: Make a note of your answers to these questions and the pages on which the information about the characters is given. These notes will be useful for activities in the final section.

Key events: These questions identify the key events that have happened and examine them in detail.

Prologue to Chapter 2

Tracking

Prologue

1   The story opens with a group of people. What time of year is it and what are they doing?

2   Douglas says that 'the story *won't* tell' who the Governess was in love with. Who do you think she was in love with? What do you think Douglas's feelings for her were?

3   What do you learn about Miles's and Flora's situation from pages 19 to 20?

4   What does the children's uncle tell the Governess that she must never do? What does this tell you about him?

Chapter 1

Note: The story is now told by the Governess as an older woman telling us what happened in her first job as a governess.

1   Mrs Grose does not wish to show her pleasure at seeing the new Governess *too* much. Why do you think this might be?

2   What two things does the Governess hear on her first night at Bly?

3   Where is Flora to sleep now that the new Governess has arrived?

4   What does the Governess hint at to Mrs Grose about her feelings towards their employer?

Chapter 2

1   A letter arrives from the children's uncle.

   a   What does it contain and how is it connected with his 'condition' of employment?

   b   How does Mrs Grose react to the letter?

2   Mrs Grose is very reluctant to tell the Governess about the first governess.

   a   What subjects, in particular, does she avoid?

   b   What connection might there be with Mrs Grose trying not to show her pleasure *too* much when she first sees the Governess?

3   Mrs Grose refers to a man who is obviously *not* the master and says that this man liked women who were 'young and pretty'.

   a   Who might this be?

   b   Why do you think Mrs Grose does not want to talk about him?

4   What do we learn about the first governess from this chapter?

Character

1   Douglas is a rather sad and serious man.

   a   Why do you think Henry James made his character like this?

   b   How does this add to the mood of the story?

2   Douglas introduces the Governess and then she tells the story from Chapter 1.

   a   What impressions do you have of her?

   b   What does the *way* she tells her story tell us about her personality?

3   Mrs Grose is described as a 'stout simple plain clean wholesome woman'. What impressions do you have of her? (Look carefully at what she says to the Governess.)

4   We have not met Miles at this point and Flora is only described briefly, but we have heard a lot about them.

a What do you know about them?

b What are your impressions of them?

Key events

1 **Douglas tells us about the Governess's life.**

Make a list of all the things you learn about the Governess from Douglas.

2 **The Governess arrives at Bly.**

What is the Governess's mood when when she arrives at Bly?

3 **The uncle's letter arrives.**

How does the letter change your impression of Miles?

CHAPTERS 3 TO 7

Tracking

Chapter 3

1 Miles has now arrived at Bly. Why does the Governess intend to do nothing about the letter from which she learns that Miles has been expelled?

2 What is going through the Governess's mind just before she sees the figure on the tower? Who, in particular, is she thinking about?

3 What hints are there in the description of the figure on the tower that he is not an ordinary visitor to Bly?

Chapter 4

1 At first, the Governess thinks that the figure on the tower might be a mad relative living secretly at Bly. She then thinks that the servants might be playing a trick on her. How does she finally explain the figure to herself?

2 How does the Governess's 'charming work' help her at this point in the story?

3 The Governess decides that the charge against Miles must be untrue. How does she come to this conclusion and what reason does she give for the school's treatment of Miles?

4 The Governess sees the figure again.

    a Where is he?

    b What is peculiar about his stare?

    c What does the Governess do when she leaves the dining-room?

    d What surprises her in Mrs Grose's reaction when she sees Mrs Grose through the window?

Chapter 5

1   The Governess says that the man she has seen is not a 'gentleman'. What does she mean by this?

2   It is only at the end of their conversation that Mrs Grose admits that she knows who the figure is. What do we learn about him and why do you think that Henry James makes Mrs Grose so reluctant to speak about what has happened at Bly?

3   What do you learn about the time when Peter Quint and the uncle were at Bly? What happened after the uncle left?

Chapter 6

1   Who does the Governess think Quint was looking for through the window?

2   Mrs Grose describes Quint as 'too free with everyone'. What does she mean by this?

3   What part does the uncle play in Quint's power over others at Bly?

4   Mrs Grose gives the Governess the impression that she had 'kept back' something when she was talking about Quint. What do you think this might have been?

5   How did Peter Quint die?

6   The Governess sees herself as having an important role in protecting the children. How will she do this?

7   The Governess becomes aware of a 'presence' by the lake. What is peculiar about Flora's behaviour at this point?

Chapter 7

1   The Governess is shocked because she thinks that the children know about the ghosts of Peter Quint and Miss Jessel.

    a What is she 'afraid of' in this situation?

    b What does she think the ghosts want?

2 Mrs Grose is still unwilling to say what happened at Bly the previous summer. Look carefully at the end of this chapter.

    a Why do you think Miss Jessel had to leave Bly?

    b How is Quint connected with this situation?

3 At the beginning of this chapter, the Governess sees herself as shielding the children from the ghosts, but at the end she says that the children are 'lost'. What do you think she means by this and in what way are they lost?

Character

1 This story is being told by the Governess a long time after the events she is describing. She describes herself as a young woman and comments on her character and in this way we can build up an idea of her personality. This is particularly true in Chapter 3. Look at the extracts below and say what you think the the Governess thinks about her younger self and what impressions you get of her character.

    a 'I found it simple, in my ignorance, my confusion, and perhaps my conceit, to assume that I could deal with a boy whose education for the world was all on the point of beginning.'

    b 'I learnt something…that had not been one of the teachings of my small smothered life; learnt to be amused, and even amusing, and not to think for the morrow.'

    c 'I used to speculate…as to how the rough future (for all futures are rough!) would handle them and might bruise them.'

    d 'It was a pleasure at these moments to feel myself tranquil and justified; doubtless perhaps also to reflect that by my discretion, my quiet good sense and general high propriety, I was giving pleasure – if he ever thought of it! – to the person to whose pressure I had yielded.'

    e 'I daresay I fancied myself…a remarkable young woman…'

2 One of the ways in which Henry James creates mystery and suspense is through the character of Mrs Grose. Mrs Grose knows what has happened at Bly before the Governess arrived but does not want to talk about it. For instance, at the end of Chapter 2 she rushes off because she does not want to tell the Governess how Miss Jessel died. In this way the writer is able to delay your discovery of the truth. Look again at the conversations between the two women in Chapters 5 and 7. Find examples in each conversation of when Mrs Grose:

    a avoids telling the truth.

    b tries to find out how much the Governess knows about Quint and Miss Jessel.

    c begins to tell the Governess about the Quint and Miss Jessel.

    d hints at what has happened without giving a full account.

Remember that Mrs Grose is not an educated woman and is one of the servants at Bly. Bearing this in mind, why do you think she was so unwilling to tell the Governess about events at Bly before her arrival?

3   In this section you meet the ghosts of both Quint and Miss Jessel and you learn about what happened before their deaths.

    a Make sure that you have a clear impression of these two characters by looking again at pages 39, 40, 45, 51–52, 55–57 and 62–65.

    b What do you learn about their:

- social background?
- physical appearance?
- personality?
- relationship?
- how they both died?

Key events

1   **The figure on the tower and at the window.**

Make sure that you know:

    a what happened just before the figure appeared and what happened directly after the figure disappeared.

    b the description of the figure.

    c the Governess's reactions to the figure and Mrs Grose's reaction to the Governess when she sees her at the window.

2   **Miss Jessel by the lake.**

Make sure that you know:

    a exactly what happened.

    b how each character reacts to the figure across the lake.

    c the Governess's thoughts about her companions.

    d how Miss Jessel is described.

CHAPTERS 8 TO 13

Tracking

Chapter 8

1   Mrs Grose tells the Governess that she tried to stop Miles and Quint being 'perpetually together'. What response to her objections does she get from:

    a Miss Jessel?

    b Miles?

2 The Governess describes Quint and Miss Jessel as 'two wretches'. Why do you think she is *so* critical of them?

3 '…while he was with the man—' 'Miss Flora was with the woman. It suited them all!'. What does Mrs Grose mean by 'it suited them all'?

Chapter 9

1 How do the children please the Governess so much in this part of the story?

2 What is the Governess doing just before she goes out of her room to the top of the stairs?

3 The Governess sees Quint on the stairs. How does Henry James create a ghostly atmosphere in this passage?

Chapter 10

1 The Governess finds Flora out of her bed on two occasions in this chapter.

    a Where is she?

    b What does the Governess think she is lying about?

    c What does the Governess think she is looking at the second time she is not in her bed?

2 Who else does the Governess see on the stairs?

3 The Governess sees Miles on the lawn in the moonlight. What is important about the fact that he is looking up at the tower?

Chapter 11

1 Why do Mrs Grose and the Governess not meet in private any more?

2 This chapter concentrates on the period following Miles's and Flora's night movements.

    a How does Miles explain his behaviour to the Governess?

    b What part does Flora play in this episode?

    c What 'trap' does the Governess suddenly realise she has fallen into?

Chapter 12

1 The Governess's attitude to the children changes in this chapter.

a What does she think they are really doing on the lawn?

b In what way does she think their 'beauty' and 'goodness' is a 'fraud'?

2 What does the Governess think the ghosts are trying to achieve?

3 What solution does Mrs Grose have for the situation and how does the Governess react to her suggestion?

Chapter 13

1 This chapter covers a period of time in the story from late summer to autumn. Read these key sentences from the chapter and think about the short questions that follow. These will enable you to gain an overall view of the chapter.

a '...it was absolutely traceable that they were aware of my predicament...'

What is the Governess's predicament at this point in the story?

b '...so much avoidance couldn't have been made successful without a great deal of tacit arrangement...'

'What I had then had an ugly glimpse of was that my eyes might be sealed just while theirs were most opened.'

The Governess suspects that the children are in communication with the ghosts and deliberately avoiding the subject with her. Why should they do this and what do they gain by it?

c 'There were times of our being together when I would have been ready to swear that, literally, in my presence, but with my direct sense of it closed, they had visitors who were known and were welcome.'

The Governess thinks that the ghosts are present when she is with the children. What attitude does she think they have towards the ghosts?

d 'What it was least possible to get rid of was the cruel idea that, whatever I had seen, Miles and Flora saw *more* – things terrible and unguessable and that sprang from dreadful passages of intercourse in the past.'

What does this tell us about what the Governess thinks the influence of the ghosts is on the children?

2 The children write letters to their uncle but the Governess does not send them. What is the connection between this and her threat at the end of Chapter 12?

Character

1   Mrs Grose is described as being 'a magnificent monument to the blessing of a want of imagination.' She is presented throughout the story as dull but solidly loyal to the Governess. The Governess, on the other hand, describes herself as having an 'infernal imagination'.

   a   In what other ways are these two characters opposites?

   b   Why is it important in the story that Mrs Grose is dull but loyal?

   c   What do you think is Mrs Grose's function in the story?

2   This section of the story deals mainly with what the Governess *thinks* the children are doing with the ghosts of Quint and Miss Jessel. She says that they are a 'fraud' and merely tricking Mrs Grose and herself into thinking that they are unaware of the ghosts. The Governess's suspicions are based on feelings and not direct proof. (Remember that (i) the Governess admits to having an 'infernal imagination', and (ii) no one else sees the ghosts, *but* (iii) Miles's explanation for being on the lawn is not very believable, and (iv) Miles and Flora never mention Quint or Miss Jessel.)

   a   How were Miles and Flora first presented by the Governess?

   b   Has her opinion changed and, if so, in what ways?

   c   Do you think the children are 'in touch' with the ghosts or is it all in the Governess's imagination?

   d   Why is the Governess afraid to ask them directly about their contact with the ghosts?

Key events

1   **Quint on the stairs and Miles on the lawn.**

   How does Henry James create an air of suspense around these two events? Look carefully at what the Governess is doing just beforehand and the mood of the writing.

2   **Miles on the lawn and Flora at the window.**

   Think about the possible reasons for the difference between the children's explanation of what they are doing and the Governess's interpretation of their actions.

CHAPTERS 14 TO 20

Tracking

Chapter 14

1   Miles asks the Governess when he is going back to school.

    a What effect does this have on her?

    b What is Miles's main reason for wanting to go back to school?

2   The Governess tells Miles that his uncle does not care very much about what happens to him. What other reason might the Governess have for not wanting Miles to write to his uncle?

Chapter 15

1   Why is the Governess so upset by Miles's request to go to school?

2   What does the Governess plan to do to avoid meeting the uncle at Bly?

3   What is Henry James hinting at in the scene where the Governess finds herself sitting in the same position on the stairs as Miss Jessel (page 108)?

4   The Governess has another encounter with Miss Jessel.

    a How is she described?

    b In what way has the Governess changed her mind afterwards?

Chapter 16

1   What does the Governess tell Mrs Grose that Miss Jessel has said to her? She may be making this conversation up – why might she do this?

2   Why do you think the Governess has changed her mind about asking the children's uncle to come to Bly?

Chapter 17

1   Miles and the Governess have a conversation about his schooling and bringing the uncle to Bly to arrange this.

    a Why are these two things difficult for the Governess?

    b What does Miles mean by 'this queer business of ours'?

    c What reason does he give for never mentioning his school or the time before he went to school?

    d Why does Miles react so violently when the Governess says 'I just want you to help me to save you!'?

Chapter 18

1   What part does Miles play when Flora goes missing?

2   What does the Governess think the children are doing while they search for Flora?

3 Why does the Governess decide to send her letter at this point?

Chapter 19

1 Why does the Governess head straight for the lake to find Flora?

2 What does the Governess mean when she describes Flora as 'not a child: she's an old, old woman'?

3 What change of expression do we see on Flora's face as she looks at the Governess?

4 What does the Governess want to know from Flora?

Chapter 20

1 Why does Miss Jessel's appearance show that the Governess is 'neither cruel nor mad'?

2 What is so striking about Flora's expression?

3 Flora says 'I see nobody' and wants to be taken away from the Governess. Why has she turned against the Governess?

4 What has been removed from the Governess's room when she returns to the house?

Character

1 Throughout the story the children's uncle is referred to as someone who will be able to sort out all the problems at Bly.

   a Look again at Chapters 14 to 16 and make a note of all the occasions on which he is mentioned.

   b For each occasion write down what they hope he will be able to do for them.

2 In fact, the uncle *never* comes to Bly and so his desire not to be disturbed is met. Even though we never see him at Bly, in what ways do you think he is an important part of the story? You might think about:

   a the Governess's feelings for him.

   b his relationship with Quint.

   c his role as the children's guardian.

3 At the end of Chapter 15, we are given the clearest picture of the ghost of Miss Jessel. She is described by the Governess in such a way that she seems evil and menacing. Look again at how she is described in

Chapters 5 to 7. She also seems to be a sad and tragic figure, especially as she is decribed sitting on the stairs. We gather that she has had an affair with Quint and has died at home giving birth to his child. For falling in love with a servant and getting pregnant, the Governess calls her evil.

a   What do you think of Miss Jessel?

b   Is she, as the Governess says 'evil' or might there be another way of looking at her character and the story behind what happens to her?

4   In Chapter 17, Miles is shown to be playful and sensitive. He makes a very reasonable request – to be sent to school so that he can be with other boys and be taught by men.

a   What are your impressions of him at this point in the story?

b   In what ways have your impressions of him changed as you have read the story?

c   Do you think the Governess has given us a fair and truthful picture of him?

Key events

In this section of the story, Henry James prepares us for the climax. The important events are:

- Flora by the lake.
- Miss Jessel in the schoolroom.
- The Governess's conversation with Miles about school.
- Miles's reaction to the Governess's plea 'to help me to save you'.
- Flora's reaction to the Governess when she points out Miss Jessel across the lake and says she's '...*there*, and you know it as well as you know me!'.

Read these passages again and the pages that follow them.

1   How do these events change the relationship between the Governess, Mrs Grose and the children?

2   Both children react violently when the Governess confronts them about the ghosts. What is the reason for this and why is it important that they both react in the same way?

3   The passage in which the Governess finds Miss Jessel in the school-room comes as a surprise in the story. How does Henry James make this an effective scene? You might think about:

a   what the Governess was thinking and doing before the scene in the schoolroom.

b the significance of the Governess sitting on the stairs before she goes into the schoolroom.

c the Governess's first thoughts on seeing a figure in her room.

d the words the Governess uses to describe Miss Jessel.

4 All of these events are crisis points in the story. Look carefully at the way Henry James uses words to make these passages extreme and frightening. For example, at the end of Chapter 17 he describes 'an extraordinary blast and chill, a gust of frozen air and a shake of the room as great, as if, in the wild wind, the casement had crashed in…a loud high shriek…terror…darkness…'

Do you find Henry James's use of language effective? Quote from the text in this section to back up your opinion.

CHAPTERS 21 TO 24

Tracking

Chapter 21

1 Flora is ill with a fever and does not want to see the Governess.

    a What does the Governess think Flora hopes will happen to her?

    b What alternative plan does the Governess produce?

2 What does the Governess hope will happen when she and Miles are alone at Bly?

3 Mrs Grose tells the Governess that she believes in the ghosts, even though she has never seen them.

    a What proof does she have that they exist?

    b Why is it so important to the Governess that Mrs Grose believes in the ghosts?

4 'If he confesses he's saved. And if he's saved—' 'Then *you* are?'. In what way will the Governess be saved?

Chapter 22

1 The servants are puzzled by why Flora and Mrs Grose have left so suddenly. How does the Governess show that she is in charge of the situation?

2 The Governess is worried about asking Miles about the ghosts. Why is she so anxious about this?

3   The Governess meets Miles in the great dining-room. What is the significance of this room in the story?

Chapter 23

1   The Governess thinks that Miles is looking through the dining room at 'something he could not see'. Why does this make her hopeful?

2   The Governess reminds Miles of the night she sat on his bed (Chapter 17). Why does this make him 'visibly nervous'?

3   Why does the Governess feel guilty about trying to get the truth out of Miles about Quint and Miss Jessel?

Chapter 24

1   What confession does Miles make?

2   The Governess realises that Miles's 'sense was sealed and his communication stopped'. Why is the Governess pleased about this?

3   Miles explains that he was expelled, not for stealing, but for because he 'said things'. What happens to prevent the Governess finding out what 'things' he said?

4   Unable to see Quint, Miles attacks the Governess in a 'white rage' and calls her a 'devil'. Why do you think he is so furious?

5   What is the cause of Miles's death at the end?

Character

1   When the Governess sees Miss Jessel at the lake, Mrs Grose calls it 'a mere mistake and a worry and a joke' but by the end of the story the Governess says that they are still 'shoulder to shoulder'. Look closely at their conversations in this section. How do they come to be friends again?

2   The Governess finds herself alone in the house with Miles and hopes that he will tell her all his secrets. Read the extracts below which describe her feelings.

    a   'It was in short by just clutching the helm that I avoided total wreck…'

    b   'So, for the benefit of whom it might concern, I paraded with a sick heart.'

    c   'How…could I make a reference [to the ghosts] without a new plunge into the hideous obscure?'

    d 'So we circled about with terrors and scruples, fighters but not daring to close.'

    e '...fighting with a demon for a human soul...'

    f '...if he *were* innocent what then on earth was I?'

What mood and state of mind is she in during these closing chapters?

Key events

The story ends in a 'show down' between the Governess and the ghost of Peter Quint. We are asked to imagine a situation in which Miles dies as they fight for his soul. The reason for Miles's expulsion from school no longer seems important in this battle between good and evil.

The tension in the final scene depends on the Governess's attempts to keep him from seeing Quint who appears and disappears at the window.

1 Make a large copy of plan below of the great dining-room and mark on your plan where each character is positioned.

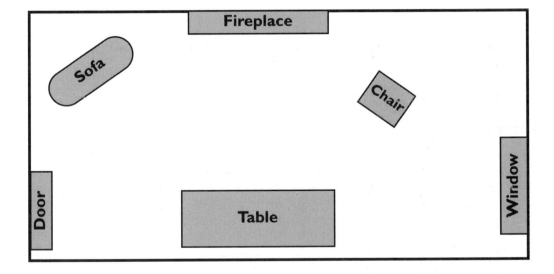

2 The Governess, Miles and Quint are described as behaving in very different ways in this chapter.

    a Copy the following table and add as many descriptions of the characters that you can from this chapter.

The Governess	Peter Quint	Miles
I sprang straight up... blind movement of getting hold of him... fell for support against the nearest piece of furniture...	...the thing at the window...its slow wheel ...the prowl of a baffled beast...	He looked in vague pain...

b As a group, act out the final scene.

LOOKING AT THE STORY AS A WHOLE

There are four aspects of *The Turn of the Screw* for you to think about in this section. They all contain topics that you will need to discuss and you are given a written task at the end of each one which is based on the points arising from your discussions.

A   Setting the scene and creating a sense of mystery

1   Henry James gives his story an introduction, the Prologue. Douglas and the other characters in the Prologue do not appear again and the Governess narrates the story to the end.

   a   Look at these sentences and, for each one, make a note about what they lead you to expect from the story.

   - 'The story had held us, round the fire, sufficiently breathless...as on a Christmas Eve in an old house a strange tale should essentially be...'
   - 'Nobody but me, till now, has ever heard. It's quite too horrible.'
   - 'For general uncanny ugliness and horror and pain.'
   - 'The story's written. It's in a locked draw – it has not been out for years.'

   b   Now think about the overall effect of the Prologue. You could make notes under the following headings:

   - The purpose of the group gathered before the fire. Look particularly at what they say when Douglas goes to bed and when he tells them about the Governess's story.
   - The location.
   - Douglas's personality.
   - The hints about who was in love.

- The delay while the story arrives from London.
- The time scale (look at the time chart on page 6).

c Look again at what Douglas tells us about the following.

- the *first* governess.
- the uncle.
- Miles, Flora and their parents.
- Bly.
- the Governess.
- Douglas's relationship with the Governess.

2 Henry James deliberately leaves out important information from the story which is about to be told.

a Make a list of all the questions that Chapter 1 makes us, as readers, want to ask.

b Why do you think Henry James leaves these questions unanswered at this stage in the story?

c The mysteries do not stop here! As the story goes on, there are several other unanswered questions, such as (i) how did Miss Jessel die? (ii) what exactly was the relationship between Quint and Miss Jessel? (iii) why does the uncle never visit them at Bly? (iv) what exactly did Miles do at school that was so dreadful? Why do you think Henry James was so mysterious in *The Turn of the Screw*?

d Talk about the questions you have listed under **a** and the points under **c** above. Think about the possible answers there might be to them. Remember that your interpretation of them is important – there will be more than one possible answer to most of them.

e Were these mysteries intriguing or annoying!

f Make a list of all the other questions you would like answers to.

Task

Imagine you are writing a letter to Henry James. In your letter you should comment on the following points:

1 How effective you think the Prologue has been, giving your reasons and quoting examples from the text.

2 Your theories about the other mysteries you have identified.

3 Whether or not these deliberate mysteries added to your enjoyment of the story.

B A story about evil

1 When *The Turn of the Screw* was first published, one newspaper called it 'the most hopelessly evil story'. This was because it presented children as being capable of evil. Miles and Flora:

   ● are under the influence of 'demon' ghosts.
   ● trick the Governess and Mrs Grose.
   ● tell lies.
   ● steal.
   ● use 'appalling language'.

   Victorian society was used to the idea that children were innocent and pure and the horror of James's story came partly from the idea that the children had been corrupted and, as the Governess says, 'lost' to the devil.

   Although the children are certainly seen by the Governess and Mrs Grose as beautiful and innocent at the beginning of the story, at one point the Governess cannot decide whether they are 'divine' or 'infernal'. However, after Miles is found on the lawn, the Governess comes to the conclusion that the children 'haven't been good – they have only been absent'.

   a Look again at the story and quote examples from the text to show how the children might have been seen as wicked.

   b At what points in the story does the Governess's attitude to the children begin to change?

   c What attitude to children in Victorian England do you think the story shows?

   d In what ways do you think attitudes to children have changed since those times?

   e Do you think Miles and Flora are divine or infernal? If two children were found to be communicating with ghosts today, do you think they would be called evil?

2 At the end of this section you will be asked to write about the subject of evil, but first you will need to think about the following points:

   a Make a list of historical figures who you consider to be evil (for example, Hitler).

   b Think of examples from recent events in the news which you would describe as acts of evil.

   c Why do you think some people are capable of being evil – is it the result of their personality or their circumstances (or a combination of both)?

   d What do you think should be done to people who commit evil acts?

e Do you think children are capable of being evil? Remember that Miles and Flora are under 10 years old.

f At one time, attempted suicide was illegal and you could be sent to prison for this 'crime'. What is your opinion of this? What crimes do you think have always been, and will always be, seen as evil by society?

Task

Write a newspaper article in which you report on a murder case in which two children have committed murder. Your article should discuss the subject of evil and include an 'expert' opinion on the subject who explains what evil is and gives his or her views on what can be done with those who commit evil acts.

C   Investigating the events at Bly

1   Imagine you are investigating rumours about the presence of ghosts at Bly, and the circumstances surrounding Miles's death.

a   In order to come to some conclusions about what has been going on, you will need to interview the following characters:

- The Governess.
- Mrs Grose.
- Flora.
- Luke (the head servant).
- the uncle.

In groups of 7 people, decide who is going to take the part of each of these characters and who will play the two investigators. The questions and answers from each interview must be recorded in a 'case file'.

b   Your investigations should include an answer to the following question:

'Was the Governess seeing ghosts which were actively trying to influence the children or was the whole thing in her imagination?'

Read the evidence below and add any of your own points before deciding if Quint and Miss Jessel were **ghosts** or **hallucinations** in the Governess's mind. The outcome of your discussions should be recorded.

Ghosts

- The Governess is convinced that she is in mortal combat with the ghosts of Miss Jessel and and Peter Quint. She decides to stay and fight the ghosts because she thinks that by doing this she will save the children from being possessed by their evil spirits.

- She thinks that the children had 'visitors who were known and welcome' and that their appearance of being good was a 'fraud'.
- She points out the figure of Miss Jessel across the lake to Flora and says 'She's there, you little unhappy thing…and you know it as well as you know me!'.
- Rather than reading to each other on the lawn, the Governess thinks that 'they're talking of *them* they're talking horrors'.
- The Governess believes that in seeing the ghosts she will 'serve as a victim and guard the tranquillity of the rest of the household. The children I should save'.

Hallucinations

- The Governess is the *only* one in the story who says she has seen the ghosts.
- Miles says that rather than talking to Quint on the tower he was only on the lawn so that she would 'think me bad for a change'.
- When the Governess discovers Flora out of bed, it is Flora who says 'You naughty: where *have* you been?'.
- At the lake, Flora denies seeing Miss Jessel: 'I see nobody, I see nothing'.
- Mrs Grose dismisses the ghosts, saying 'It's all a mere mistake and a worry and a joke'.
- The Governess admits to having 'an infernal imagination'.
- She has just been thinking about a handsome young man before she sees Quint on the tower for the first time, and so it is possible that she was only seeing the 'handsome' Quint in her imagination.

Task

Using the evidence you have gathered in the activities above, act out a courtroom scene in which your prime suspect is on trial for the murder of Miles. This scene must include:

- a judge.
- the prosecution counsel.
- the defence counsel.
- a jury.
- the witnesses.

D Class and society

The Governess always refers to Quint and Miss Jessel as if they were wicked and evil:

- 'two wretches'.
- 'unmistakable horror and evil'.
- 'dishonoured and tragic'.
- 'his white face of damnation'.
- 'the author of our woe'.

The Governess's hatred of the 'ghosts' comes partly from the influence she thinks they have over the children. However, it is possible to see this hatred in another way.

Read page 65 again. In this conversation it is hinted that Miss Jessel dies while giving birth to Quint's child. We also gather that Miss Jessel was a 'lady' and that Quint was 'dreadfully below'. Quint and Miss Jessel have therefore broken two very important social rules in Victorian society:

- They have made love before being married.
- They are from different social classes (Quint is a servant and Miss Jessel is educated and socially above him).

It is for these reasons that the Governess is so harsh about the dead man and woman. (In fact, the Governess may be jealous of Miss Jessel as she too dreams of being in love – with the children's uncle.) The problem for Miss Jessel, and all Victorian Governesses, was that she did not really belong in any social group. Governesses were not servants because they were educated and came from middle-class (but not wealthy) families – the Governess's father was a vicar – but they worked in big houses where the owners were socially above them. The affair between Quint and Miss Jessel would have meant that she was no longer a 'respectable' woman and would have no place in society.

Task

Write the story of Quint and Miss Jessel's relationship from Miss Jessel's point of view. Choose one of the following forms to tell the story:

- A diary from four different points in the relationship.
- A play in five scenes.
- A monologue.